DATE DUE	
AUG 17 1998	

Y0-CSH-985

THE GOURMET CUPID

THE GOURMET CUPID

•

Mary Fanjoy Reid

AVALON BOOKS
THOMAS BOUREGY AND COMPANY, INC.
401 LAFAYETTE STREET
NEW YORK, NEW YORK 10003

© Copyright 1998 by Mary Fanjoy Reid
Library of Congress Catalog Card Number: 98-96224
ISBN 0-8034-9302-9
All rights reserved.
All the characters in this book are fictitious,
and any resemblance to actual persons,
living or dead, is purely coincidental.

PRINTED IN THE UNITED STATES OF AMERICA
ON ACID-FREE PAPER
BY HADDON CRAFTSMEN, BLOOMSBURG, PENNSYLVANIA

To my mother for cooking me wonderful, nutritious meals; and to my father for buying the dessert.

Chapter One

The words "restructuring" and "company downsizing" were buzzing in Hally's head as she strode down the hall to Serina Heineault's office. Suddenly, the streamlined Art Deco decor took on a new, crisp chilliness, and she could feel a faint trembling beginning deep in the pit of her stomach. Hally buttoned her suit jacket, smoothed down the sleeves, and ran her hand over her long French braid as she approached the double glass doors. Serina Heineault's name was etched in silver below the Necessitas logo. Hally hadn't been called up to the fourth floor since landing the Ecron Radio account last April—and that was to celebrate.

Was Necessitas in trouble? Hally wondered queasily as she stepped inside.

The woman at the desk looked up from her computer and gave her a perfunctory smile. "Good morning, Miss Chrisswell. Mrs. Heineault is expecting you. Please, go right in."

Was that sympathy she detected in the assistant's eyes? Beads of sweat prickled beneath Hally's arms. *Keep your head up. Confidence. Poise,* she reminded herself.

"Thank you," she said, forcing her lips into a calm smile.

Serina Heineault was facing the window, talking on the telephone. Behind her, with its linear, graceful Gothic portals, loomed the Milwaukee Performing Arts Center.

Hally thought back to her own tiny office, which she happened to share with two copywriters on the first floor, and whose view included a large, uninteresting cement parking lot.

"Right . . . The proposal's being faxed to you as we speak. . . . Wonderful! . . ." She swiveled around, noticed Hally, and made a greeting gesture, indicating that Hally should sit down. ". . . Yes, tomorrow . . . Fine, yes . . . one o'clock . . . perfect. . . ."

Hally sat down, crossed her legs, then uncrossed them. She unbuttoned her jacket and laced her fingers together. Wincing at the clammy feel of her palms, she quickly wiped them on her skirt. As she did this she glimpsed a tiny hole in the knee of her stockings. Instinctively, her hand moved to conceal it. She mentally urged herself to relax, concentrating on her breathing, willing the muscles in her back to untighten.

"I'll be with you in a second, Hally." The woman behind the desk scribbled something in her date book, her long wide mouth turned slightly downward in concentration. She glanced up at Hally, her dark kohl-lined eyes smiling, her straight black hair pulled tightly away from her angular face.

And Hally was again struck with awe—as she was each time she saw Serina Heineault—by the porcelain beauty of this woman's seemingly ageless face. Beneath the flawless skin, a chalky contrast to the heavily made-up eyes and deep red lips, one would never suspect that this managing partner of Necessitas had another life apart from work: a more mundane life complete with children's dirty laundry, parent-teacher's meetings, baby-sitter problems, and home-cooked meals.

Serina Heineault put down her pen and folded her hands in front of her, focusing her dark brown eyes on Hally. "It's nice to see you, Hally. How is everything? I hear you and Wade Buchner made great strides in the

Nobler Kitty Litter account presentation." She turned to her computer, pressed a key, and stared at the screen.

"Yes, we got that account. We also still have Franco Shelving and the, uh, Milwaukee Scents accounts." Hally struggled to quell her embarrassment; to Serina Heineault these accounts must appear rather puny and insignificant. "Right now we're working on the Grantham Printing presentation—"

"Hmm... yes, I wanted to talk to you about that. Would you like some coffee? Tea?"

Hally swallowed back the dryness in her throat. Was she taking her off the account? "Yes, er, tea would be nice." She knew Serina didn't drink coffee.

Serina ordered tea on the intercom. After a moment she shifted her gaze from the computer screen back to Hally.

"I've been going over your personal file, Hally," she said, smiling. "You're not married."

"No," said Hally. Was marriage now a new employee requirement?

"No doubt you've heard about Wade Buchner."

Wade Buchner was their team's advertising executive. Hally had only learned this morning he was taking two weeks' leave of absence.

"His wife's due in a few days." Serina sighed. "I suspect he's more nervous about this baby than she is. But then, this is their first—" She exhaled a wistful breath. "I remember when I was pregnant with Teddy. Rudy practically camped outside this office. Wouldn't let me do anything. I lifted a pen and he got anxious." She chuckled.

The assistant swept into the room with the tea. As was the custom, it was served from an English Brown Betty teapot and poured into china mugs—Royal Albert, no less. When it came to Necessitas, Serina spared no expense; she, as did the other partners, believed in quality—the very best quality.

"Ahh . . . Connie, you're a lifesaver," said Serina, immediately reaching for the cream jug. Hally didn't tell her she didn't take cream—or sugar, after the managing partner of Necessitas had already dumped a generous spoonful into each mug.

After Connie closed the door, Serina proceeded to pour the tea. "I swear fall is getting shorter and shorter. Here it is not yet November, and it feels like winter is already fast approaching. I keep expecting to see snow out there." She sipped her tea and leaned back in her chair, her hands wrapped around the mug as if to warm herself.

Perspiration gathered at the small of Hally's back. Her fingers made sweaty imprints about the china mug's handle. She nodded. "Yes, uh, Christmas is just around the bend," she blurted, wincing immediately at her pathetic attempt at small talk. Normally, she was very good at this, but this woman was making her nervous. She was eager to know what this was all about. *Why doesn't Serina just come out with it?* she thought, tugging on her earlobe.

"Christmas! I don't want to even *think* about Christmas! Goodness! A parent's nightmare." Serina rolled her eyes heavenward. She looked at Hally. "Well, you don't have to worry about that, do you?"

No, she wasn't married, and she didn't have children. But back when Hally'd been hired by Necessitas—going on eleven years now—that hadn't been a prerequisite for her copywriting job. Was the company's policy changing? Was this a new nineties, or perhaps a turn-of-the-century, policy they were implementing?

"You were promoted to art director last year," said Serina, glancing back at the computer. She punched a few keys. "Wade tells me you've been doing an excellent job. You're satisfied with your team?"

"Yes," Hally answered without thinking. "Danny and Marla are terrific copywriters. We work very well together." Her words sifted out of her mouth as if she were reading from a TelePrompTer. She groaned inwardly and sipped her tea to keep herself from blurting out anything else. The last thing she wanted to do was put Danny and Marla's jobs in jeopardy.

"Good. Good," said Serina absently. "Because I'm taking you and your team off the Grantham Printing account, and handing it over to Robert Thompson's people."

Hally gulped, her tongue suddenly growing thick in her mouth.

"I'm putting you on the Bel Abner account instead."

"Bel Abner?" Hally croaked, blinking in disbelief. That was a major account. She'd heard Bel Abner Gourmet Products was shopping around for new advertising representation, but—

"I'm aware that you've not had much experience handling presentations as big as this, Hally—but I have faith in you." Serina flashed her a reassuring smile. "And... well, truthfully? This is a bad time for everyone, it seems." She sighed. "Shawn Kienzel is busy with Wainscott Warehouse and the new Brookner account. And Dana Bradford's got some, er, family problems. Two members of Max Caine's team are on maternity leave, and, well..."

...*I'm single and I have no personal obligations,* thought Hally.

"I've been reading through your personal file. And what do you know? It says here that gourmet cooking just happens to be one of your passions." Serina grinned, shaking her head. "Not often does this kind of luck drop into my lap. It didn't take me long, Hally, to see you are the perfect person to handle this account."

Hally's hands turned ice cold even as she clutched the steaming china mug tightly. *That personal file is eleven years old!* she wanted to protest. It was true—at the time—she'd wanted to learn gourmet cooking. But then projects and deadlines got in the way, and she'd never really had the time to enroll in cooking classes—

"The Bel Abner file will be downloaded to your office later this morning," Serina told her.

"But Wade—"

"In the meantime, I've decided to appoint you as acting Advertising Executive on this one, Hally. Congratulations."

She caught Hally's stunned reaction. "Now, I wouldn't do this if I didn't think you could handle the account, Hally. You've been an art director for over a year now, isn't that right? And you've been working as a copywriter for what—?" She consulted the computer monitor. "Nearly ten years? Well, Hally, you've certainly been an asset to this company, and I want you to know that we appreciate your hard work. I think you'll do a terrific job."

She rose from her chair and came around the desk as Hally stood, unsteadily, her head reeling with uncertainty. Serina led her to the door.

"Remember." She patted Hally's hot shoulder, then put her hand to her own heart. "Let it come from here. The heart is the strongest, most willful muscle in the body, after all. The head and the gut, okay sure, they come into play, as well. But the heart, that's where the good ideas come from."

Serina's dark red lips curved upward in a coy smile, a subtle artfulness glittering in her dark eyes. "Of course, a pretty face and an impeccable wardrobe won't do any harm."

Hally's hand quickly moved to conceal the hole in her stockings.

"And let's not forget who we are: Necessitas, the goddess who presides over the destinies of mankind; 'Mother of the three Fates.'" Serina gave a good-natured laugh; she'd been one of the founders of Necessitas, and had penned that slogan herself.

Connie opened the door and poked her head in. "Serina? Your son Teddy's on line one. Says it's urgent."

"When is it not?" Serina sighed. "Well, there goes one of my three Fates." She shook Hally's hand. "Congratulations, Hally. I know you and your team will do Necessitas proud—Oh! I forgot." She put her arm around Hally's shoulders. "You've probably heard about Randall and Deliah Abner...I mean about their little quirks, right? They tend to be quite particular about, er, certain details." Serina paused, gazing past Hally distractedly.

"The Abners," she went on after a moment, "you see, are partial to intimate presentations. People tend to overlook this fact, and Deliah Abner has more influence in company decisions than people think. And suddenly this brilliant idea came to me!"

Hally waited, not sure she wanted to hear this "brilliant idea" of Serina's.

"What I thought, Hally, well—why don't you present the concept sketches and comps at your apartment. And then that'll give you the opportunity to cook up one of your fabulous gourmet meals—using their products, of course." She chuckled. "It's perfect, isn't it?"

"Yes, perfect," Hally echoed hollowly.

She strode woodenly out of the office, leaving the managing partner satisfied and hopeful, with Hally herself a little stunned, her anxiety and agitation growing with each step.

I think I'm in trouble, she groaned to herself.

As she passed through the glass doors, Hally heard a low wolf whistle follow her from the waiting area. Indignance rose in her even as she heard Connie address the whistler before the glass doors closed behind her:

"Mrs. Heineault wasn't expecting you, but she'll be with you as soon as she can, Mr. Abner."

Hally froze in her tracks. Mr. Abner? Her indignance swiftly dissipated, and her expression brightened, transforming immediately into abrupt attentiveness. What luck! She would go back into the reception room and introduce herself. Her hand went to her tight French braid—not a hair out of place. She straightened her suit blazer and ran her tongue over her teeth. *Confidence, Hally.*

But her head was still muzzy with Serina's unexpected news, and there was a nervous fluttering taking over her stomach. She eyed the hole in the knee of her stocking. No, first impressions meant everything in this business, and she didn't want to mess up the campaign before it even got off the ground.

I'm not ready yet, anyway, she thought dismally. Not for a second did Hally doubt she could handle this temporary promotion to advertising executive, but she needed a little time to let it all sink in.

And she also needed to learn how to cook—gourmet food, no less. She grimaced, tugging hard on her earlobe, trying to clear her head so she could think of a way to salvage the situation.

"Gee, you mean you lied on your résumé?" said Danny, wide-eyed.

"Remember that guy—Lenny Bryce? Didn't he get fired for telling them he graduated from Green Bay, or something?" said Marla.

"Thanks, Marla. I needed to hear that." Now Hally was regretting bringing this up. But she trusted these

The Gourmet Cupid   9

two; she had to. "Hey, this goes no further than this room, right?" Hally rubbed the back of her neck. "Besides, it wasn't really a *lie*, per se. I did intend to take some cooking classes. I mean, it's not as if I lied about my educational background."

Danny and Marla exchanged doubtful glances.

"So, we have four weeks. I'll—I'll just . . . enroll in some cooking classes."

"It's, uh, kind of short notice, don't you think?" said Marla. "Those kind of specialty classes fill up pretty quick, and I think a lot of them have already started . . ."

Hally held her head in her hands, groaning aloud.

"Well, Bel Abner would be the biggest account we ever worked on, and if we want to land this account—" began Danny. But he didn't bother to finish the statement. He gazed up at Hally, shrugging.

Hally sighed, peering at them between her splayed fingers. "Well? Any suggestions?"

Danny wheeled his chair back to his drawing table. "We'd better get cooking," he said, grinning.

Hmmm . . . I think we might already be cooked, Hally added silently. But even as she thought this, she was remembering that wolf whistle that had followed her out of the reception room.

She'd assumed the whistler had been a younger man; however, the Bel Abner file put Randall Abner at sixty-four, married forty-two years. And yet, Hally supposed that even an older, happily married man could still very well appreciate a "pretty face and impeccable wardrobe"; Serina Heineault might be right about that, at least.

Hally glanced down at the tiny hole in her stocking that had now gaped open to reveal her entire kneecap. She gritted her teeth and made a mental reminder to herself to make sure she wore extra-strength stockings that day.

* * *

"Tina, you've got to help me! Every place I've called, their cooking courses have already started, or they're not beginning until December. And we're scheduled to do this presentation the end of November."

"You can't postpone it?"

Hally exhaled a long-suffering breath into the phone receiver. "There are three other firms competing with Necessitas for this account. By the time I learn how to cook they'll have already decided to go with someone else."

A beat passed. "Okay, hold on a sec. I just remembered something I read the other day..."

Hally waited impatiently, listening to the rustle of papers in the background. Finally, Tina came back on the phone:

"Here it is! You're lucky I don't throw anything out. Last week's *Milwaukee Heartbeat*. Now, lessee..."

"*Milwaukee Heartbeat*? Isn't that a singles' magazine?"

"Hey, motherhood tends to make you nostalgic for the good ol' days. You know, when I was wild and single." Tina sighed wistfully. "Not that I'd ever give up my husband or the twins," she quickly added.

"There's nothing 'wild' about my life," muttered Hally.

"Okay. This is it: 'Passion for Gourmet with Lou Jay.'" Tina read over the phone. "Kinda catchy, don't you think? Listen to this: 'Spice up your love life and cook yourself into your lover's heart. Heat up the kitchen and say it all with Gourmet.'"

"Oh, no" moaned Hally. "Tina, that sounds like a personal ad. I can just imagine the kind of people who would enroll in a course like that—"

"People who stay home alone in their apartment on weekends. People who bring their work home with them on Friday, and spend the evening working and defrosting a frozen meal," said Tina. "People like you, Hally."

It did sound like her, thought Hally. "I don't know..."

"It's perfect, Hally. The first class begins this Friday. And think of it: not only will you be learning how to cook gourmet meals, but you might actually meet the man of your dreams."

Hally kneaded her temples. The man of her dreams. Right. At present she had more pressing matters to deal with than romance. "Okay. Give me the number," she finally relented.

When she hung up, she paused for a moment to collect her thoughts. How much was she going to learn in four weeks, anyway? Twelve classes surely wouldn't make her a gourmet connoisseur. What could she have been thinking? It took years of experience to prepare a gourmet meal—and she had trouble boiling an egg.

But then, all she had to do was make *one* meal—one fabulous, unforgettable meal. She could do that, surely? Her whole adult life, Hally had never really taken an interest in cooking, never made an effort to learn how to cook. And Tina was right about the frozen dinners; Hally was Queen of the Defrosters. Defrosting: that was pretty much the extent of Hally's culinary expertise.

However, was she really ready to stick herself in a class full of single people looking for mates? A dozen people all hungry for love?

Hally sighed, and relentingly picked up the phone. She dialed the number on the pad in front of her.

"Hallo! Lou Jay, Chef Gourmet," the voice on the other end chanted.

"Uh, I was wondering . . . if it's not too late, that is— if I could, er, sign up for your, er, cooking class."

"No! No! Never too late for Gourmet!" the voice answered quickly. "Ah! And as fate would have it, I am in need of one more student to balance the symmetry. Please, what is your name, Miss?"

Hally hesitated, rubbing her face uncertainly. "Balance the symmetry"? What was that supposed to mean, exactly?

"Love and Gourmet, they are like two links in a chain, no? And you—I can hear it in your voice—you have a gourmet heart."

"Gourmet heart"? There was a salesmanlike pitch to the way he said this. But too, she heard in his voice a strange kind of sincerity—this was a man who truly believed in what he was saying.

Did she want to do this? She winced. But then, did she really have a choice?

"Hallo? Miss? Miss? Are you still there, Miss?"

"Yes," Hally managed with a surrendering sigh. She slumped forward on her desk, the phone still to her ear.

"Sign me up."

"So let me get this straight. You're inviting the Abners—Randall and Deliah Abner of Bel Abner Gourmet Foods—to *your* apartment?" Tina poured more coffee into Hally's mug.

Little Gloria climbed up on the sofa and nestled in under Hally's arm. Hally moved her cup to the other hand just as Rory leaped up and snuggled his curly head under her other arm.

"You sure you don't want any wine?" Tina held up the bottle, grinning. "Wine is an important part of the gourmet meal, you know. It provides that added romantic ambience. And you, of all people, should know that romance sells in advertising."

"You have a one-track mind, Tina," grumbled Hally. But she was thinking about what the man on the phone had said earlier. Love and gourmet; linking these two concepts together seemed ridiculous to her. What was so

The Gourmet Cupid 13

romantic about getting all hot and sweaty over a hot stove?

"Well, I took your suggestion and signed up for that cooking class." Hally sighed. "But I don't know about this Lou Jay guy. On the phone he sounded a bit... odd."

Tina sipped her wine, her expression thoughtful. "You're definitely going to have, to do something about that apartment of yours. It's, well—if you don't mind me saying—a little too... sterile."

"Sterile? What do you mean? Just because it's clean and tidy—"

Tina's dark brown eyes lit up. "Hey! I could come over and help you redecorate. Maybe paint the walls, hang a few interesting prints?"

Hally glanced at the toy Lego set strewn across her friend's living room, the teddy bears and miniature cars, the wadded-up Kleenex and empty plastic cups and straws dotting the room. "Gee, Tina. I don't want to put you out—"

"No, no. I'd love to do it!" Tina's heart-shaped face flushed with excitement. She set down her wineglass. "I've been dying to do something, you know—constructive." She gazed at the twins, dozing comfortably on either side of Hally. "I mean, don't get me wrong, I love motherhood, I do. But a part of me yearns to get back out there in the work force. Well, look at you. Your life is so interesting and exciting."

"Interesting? Exciting? Tina, I'm a basket case half the time. I work fifty, sixty hours a week. And now, with this new account, with the managing partners believing I can cook—" Hally kneaded her brow. "Okay, so I'm finally making some real money for a change, but I don't have anyone special to spend it on, to go out to dinner with—"

"Roger Chetner," interrupted Tina.

"Who?"

"He's an insurance broker. He works with Garry," said Tina. "Don't worry, he's not affiliated with Serina or Rudy Heineault. I know how you like to keep your work and private life separate."

Hally groaned. "Tina, you know how I feel about blind dates."

"Oh, this guy's not blind," said Tina, grinning. Upon seeing her friend's impatient look, she quickly added: "Okay, he's single and he's cute—and he makes a good living. What more do you want?"

That was always the niggling question. What did she want? From that first day she'd met Tina, eleven years ago at the Heineaults' annual summer barbecue (Rudy Heineault and Garry were old college roommates), Tina had taken it upon herself to search out "suitable" bachelors for Hally. But all her attempts at matchmaking failed miserably. Hally had already conceded she was already married to her work. However, Tina was not willing to give up that easily.

"You're no spring chicken, you know, Hally," Tina pointed out. "If you keep fooling around like this, all the eligible men will have already been picked over. You'll find yourself scraping the bottom of the barrel, Hal. My advice is to grab them now, while you still can."

"You make it sound like some kind of shopping spree—like I'm at the market selecting tomatoes from a fruitcart, or something." Hally leaned back against the sofa wearily, and both Gloria and Rory burrowed closer, sucking their thumbs contentedly.

"And you've got a way with kids, Hally. Like it or not, you're a family girl at heart." Tina shook her head. "I know how important your career is to you. But in the end, what have you got? A great retirement package, and no one to share it with." A tender glow crossed her face, and she smiled, that same contented smile that appeared on the twins' sleeping faces. "You know, love is definitely underrated. I just wish you could find—"

"Well, hello, girls!" Garry strode in and set down his briefcase, yawning. He took off his coat, and walked over to Tina, kissing her. "Hi ya, pumpkin."

"Long meeting?" she inquired, even as the twins awoke and immediately dashed over to their father.

Garry smiled despite his weariness, and scooped them both up in his arms. "Whoa! You two've got to stop eating all those peanut butter and banana sandwiches!"

"Silly Daddy! We had macaroni and cheese for dinner!" They giggled.

Garry smiled at Hally. "Hi, Hally. How's the advertising business treatin' ya?"

"It appears to be driving me into the kitchen," she muttered almost inaudibly. Sighing, she consulted her watch. "Speaking of which, I'd better get going. I still have a ton of work to get through tonight."

"Hally's working on a new account—Bel Abner Gourmet Products," Tina told him. "Hal's an advertising executive now."

"*Acting* Advertising Executive," Hally amended, rising.

"Bel Abner, eh? I thought I just read something about them." Garry frowned, then suddenly snapped his fingers. "Oh, right! Actually, it was about *Benton* Abner—Randall Abner's eldest son. Apparently, he was in some bachelor auction or something just recently. Raised over forty thousand dollars for some charity or other. Broke a record."

Tina's brows lifted. "Oh, really?"

Hally knew that look. "Tina—" she began, with a warning glare.

"So the Abners have a bachelor son, eh? Interesting

... So what's this Benton Abner like? Handsome and charming, I'll bet."

Garry chuckled. He was well apprised of his wife's matchmaking plans for Hally. "The society pages paint him as the 'black sheep of the family.' A bit of a rebel, I guess. But it seems he has women falling all over him. It was rumored he was once engaged to Veronica Wilmott."

Tina gasped, impressed. "You mean the television actress?" She tapped her chin, her expression suddenly turning thoughtful. "So . . . he dates only actresses?"

Garry gazed at his wife. "He's number nine on America's Most Eligible Bachelor list—or whatever they call it." He scratched his head. "Now, where'd I read that? I remember it was a big article in a magazine . . ."

"In any case, this means Benton Abner hasn't met that special someone yet," said Tina, glancing over at Hally, that familiar plotting look creeping into her expression.

Hally pursed her lips together. "As far as I know," she said, "Benton Abner doesn't directly involve himself in the family business."

"Well, that could easily be rectified, couldn't it? Why, you could invite him over for your incredible gourmet dinner!" Tina suggested. "Because everyone knows that the way to a man's heart is through the stomach."

"You know, I never understood that," said Hally, exchanging glances with Garry, who shrugged, equally bemused.

"I didn't know you could cook, Hally," he said. The twins wiggled in his arms and he let them down.

"I can't," said Hally glumly.

Garry looked more confused.

"Can we come over for dinner, Aunt Hally?" asked Rory, running over to clasp her hand. "Please?"

"You like frozen dinners, then?" She tousled his hair playfully.

Garry ushered the children to bed. "Well, we'll see you Saturday night, right?" Rory and Gloria beckoned to him from the top of the stairs. "Okay! I'm coming!" And he bounded up the stairs, chasing them as they gamboled down the hallway, shrieking with delight.

Hally slipped on her coat. "Saturday night?"

Tina ran her tongue over her teeth, her lips moving into an almost imperceptible grimace. "Uh, yes. I didn't mention it? You're coming here for dinner Saturday night."

Hally's eyes narrowed in sudden suspicion. "Oh? Dare I ask the nature of this dinner?"

"Okay, now don't get angry." Tina imitated a calming gesture with her hands. "But I invited Roger Chetner over."

"Who?"

"You know, the insurance salesman I was telling you about? Well, anyway, I thought that if I invited the two of you over for dinner—"

"Oh, no! I'm not being set up again." Hally stepped over the toys strewn across the floor, and slalomed into the hall. "You can count me out."

"Aw, give it a chance, Hally. Roger's a great guy once you get to know him," Tina implored. "And you know, the holidays are coming up. Who're you going to spend Thanksgiving with? And what about Christmas? New Year's? Your work can only keep you company for so long, you know."

Hally turned and wrapped her plaid scarf about her neck with a resolute flourish. She pulled on her gloves and flexed the fingers. "I'm fine, Tina. Really, I am. I'm happy about the way things are. A relationship would only... complicate things. And besides, right now, I need to focus all my attention on making it through this Bel Abner presentation."

"And maybe, in the meantime, you'll run into Benton

Abner," said Tina, opening the door. She returned Hally's glare with an innocent look. "Well, you never know— Oh! And about redecorating your apartment. Why don't you drop by... oh, say Saturday night? We'll go over some ideas, okay?"

Hally walked down the front steps. She sighed. "Yeah, sure." She gave a brief wave and strode briskly toward her dark blue Mustang parked beneath the streetlight.

It wasn't until she was in her car and speeding down the road, that she realized she'd just committed herself to another one of Tina's blind-date setups.

But as she nosed her Mustang past the Milwaukee County Zoo, and veered left on 124th Street toward her apartment building, Hally found her thoughts drifting to the phone call she'd made earlier that day.

That strange man, Lou Jay, had called her a "Gourmet Heart." What had she set herself up for? she thought, cringing. He'd mentioned the words "gourmet" and "love" an awful lot, and together in the same sentence as if they were interchangeable. She needed to learn how to cook; she wasn't looking for love. But now, Hally had the sneaking suspicion that she hadn't enrolled in a cooking class, but had answered a personal ad.

There was something else eating at her. She hadn't mentioned it to Tina or Garry, but in the Abner file, Benton Abner's name had popped up more than a few times. He and his younger brother, Stewart, held a substantial percentage of stock in the Bel Abner Gourmet Company, and Benton was, just this past year, instated as an active member on the board. Hally tugged on her earlobe, grimacing in thought; business protocol required her to extend Benton Abner an invitation to the presentation.

But why should this make her nervous? It was only a business dinner, after all—and so what if Benton Abner was number nine on the most eligible bachelor list? How handsome and charming could he be? And even if he was, that didn't mean she'd immediately fall head over heels in love with him.

No, Hally was content with her life; she'd found all the excitement and fulfillment she needed in her current position as art director—and now, as acting advertising executive. She let the latter title roll off her tongue, savoring the taste of it. If she managed to land this account she might very well acquire that title for real.

She gripped the wheel, smiling proudly to herself, ignoring the small feeling of anxiety worrying itself somewhere deep in the pit of her stomach. Yes, she was a woman on the move—a career woman, she told herself. She glanced up at her reflection in the rearview mirror.

Romance would just have to wait; for at the moment, there was no room left in her heart for love.

Chapter Two

Nowhere in the Bel Abner file could Hally find any photographs of Benton Abner, and much to her chagrin, she found herself feeling strangely disappointed over this fact.

"Research department dropped off those figures you wanted," said Danny, motioning toward her desk without looking up from his copy.

But what Hally wanted wasn't financial figures. For the past week she'd cloaked herself in Bel Abner's business and financial history, and in the process, had inadvertently discovered some surprises and matters of interest concerning the "black sheep of the family": Benton Abner. Normally, Hally wasn't one to listen to gossip, or snoop into people's personal lives, but for once, her curiosity was strong enough to shuffle aside her professional sense of propriety.

"Marla? What's that magazine called—uh, you know, the one that names the top twenty eligible bachelors?" Hally picked up one of the computer printouts, and drawing her brows together, she pretended to scan the tables of figures.

"Oh, you mean *People* magazine? Or, probably you're thinking of *Life Worth Living*; they're always doing those kinds of profiles. You know—" Marla batted her eyelashes and puckered her lips in a dramatic but exaggerated gesture. "—stuff like 'The World's Most Beautiful Women,' 'North America's Greatest Legs,'

'Hollywood's Prettiest Nose.' Last month it was 'America's Wealthiest Bachelors and Divorcées,' " said Marla.

"You're not still holding out for 'Mister-Moneybags, let-me-take-you-away-from-all-this,' are you?" said Danny, gazing over at his coworker with a teasing grin.

Marla looked indignant. "Gord does very well as a travel agent, thank you," she retorted huffily. "And besides, I could never marry someone just for his money. Frankly, I don't know how some of these women can do it. I mean, commiting yourself to a relationship without love, without passion—"

"Susie married me for my money, of course."

The irony in Danny's words and the meaningful look he tossed Hally did not elude her. She winced; she understood all too well.

"So we have to forfeit our Christmas bonuses this year—" Hally turned up her palms in a gesture of open-mindedness. "But hey! If we manage to land this account, we're not only looking at raises, but a team promotion."

"We'll never steal Bel Abner away from Prentice & Dreyer," said Marla dejectedly. She looked as though they'd already been thwarted and outmaneuvered by this well-known, successful advertising company, their major competitor.

Hally snorted. "We don't have to *steal* this account from any other agency. Just because Prentice & Dreyer are handling the larger Milwaukee brewery campaigns doesn't mean we have less of a chance to snag this particular account," she reassured them. "And we might have one good thing going for us," she added with a smile.

"What's that?" asked Danny.

Hally let out a breath, tugging on her earlobe distractedly. "The Abners—Randall and Deliah Abner are in Venice right now."

"You mean we've got an extension?" A hopeful expression lit up Marla's face. "Because you know, I have all these plans for my wedding, and then there's the holidays coming up, and Gord's parents—"

"No," Hally interrupted her with a wince. "No extension. I was thinking, rather, about all those pre-meetings, the client conferences, lunches and cocktails—you know, all that public relations schmoozing Wade always took care of." Hally rubbed her hands together. "Yes, we're a great creative team, but when it comes to that particular end of business—"

"Wait a sec. Are we freewheeling this deal?" said Danny in alarm. He frowned. "You don't mean to say—"

"There won't be any contact with the Abners before the presentation," Hally filled in for him.

Danny's frown deepened. "This is highly irregular."

Hally shrugged; this "irregularity" made her new role as advertising executive a heck of a lot easier.

"But we need to know what Bel Abner wants," protested Marla. "How on earth can we come to an agreement on advertising strategies . . ." Her words trailed off, even as Hally observed that familiar look of panic surface into Marla's small, pert face—that nervous energy the copywriter had been carrying around her for the past month.

And Hally once again patted herself on the back for keeping her head and heart clear of any romantic interference; for she'd seen the toll the planning of this wedding had taken on this young copywriter.

However, Hally was concerned about the competition, and she knew Danny was thinking the same. Prentice & Dreyer were too large and prestigious a company to let this opportunity slip by them. Their aggressive campaign policies would no doubt include a strategic "visit" to Venice. She, herself, wouldn't have minded a vacation in sunny Italy, but their budget had already come through, and there had been no allotment in it for any travel expense outside the country. And then there was this cooking class...

"There's no chance you'll be flying to Venice, then?" Danny said this more as a grudging statement than a question. He tossed his pencil in the air and pushed back the hair from his forehead so that it stuck up straight.

Hally shook her head. She glanced at the clock on the far wall. Her first gourmet cooking class was in four hours. She tugged on her earlobe, trying to quell the frustrated excitement rising in her chest. Earlier this morning she'd checked out some books from the library. She'd scanned some of the gourmet recipes, but unfortunately had no time to absorb anything that might give her a head start on the course.

Who was she kidding? She was no cook. The man on the phone had called her a "Gourmet Heart," but then, he didn't know her. He didn't know she'd once blown up a microwave; he didn't know about the first (and only) cake she'd baked—a chocolate zucchini angel food cake which had dented the hood of her date's car; he didn't know about that one brave evening she'd attempted to cook a chicken casserole and had broken a tooth trying to eat it. No, she was pretty much a dud in the kitchen.

She tugged on her earlobe, as if to draw strength from it. "I'm going to need some newspaper clippings—magazine articles featuring the Abners," Hally announced out loud. "And a copy of last month's *Life Worth Living*."

Marla put the phone receiver to her chest and gestured to Hally. "I'm going to have to take off a little early today." She pointed at the phone in her hand and made a face. "I'm having trouble with the florist."

Hally shot the copywriter a look of exasperation. She

exhaled and compressed her lips into a patient, strained smile. She glanced over at Danny, who grimaced apologetically.

"I've got to pick up my son from hockey practice at five-thirty," he told her.

And Hally had to make her way to Humboldt Lodge by six. But then, Fridays were always moot days. Now, Monday and Wednesday evenings would be lost as well—all because of this darned cooking course, she sighed to herself. Somewhere in between they'd somehow have to manage to get this presentation up and running.

"Okay," she conceded with a shrug, "so we'll work through the weekend." Hally noted their stricken looks.

"We're taking the kids to my folks' place in Cedarsburg this weekend—"

"Gord and I have an appointment with the caterers Saturday, and Gord's brother is flying down from Duluth—"

And I have a date Saturday night, Hally suddenly remembered with an inward groan.

"Okay, okay," she relented, throwing up her hands. "Let's just get those creative juices flowing. Marla? Can you pick up some of those Bel Abner products on your way to the florist tonight?"

"I can't. Gord and I have to meet with the priest. I'm converting to Catholicism, remember?" Marla massaged her neck. "Who knew getting married would be so much trouble?"

"You should've taken my advice and eloped," smirked Danny. "Hah! Just wait till you have kids."

Hally sighed back in her chair and picked up the phone, punching in the extension for the research department. Again she gave silent thanks to her nonexistent love life. The complications rising from these gourmet cooking classes were about all she could handle at the moment.

And yet, as she relayed her requests to the man at the other end of the phone line, Hally felt a faint nagging sensation pushing against her ribs, a feeling that made her heart beat a little more quickly and her stomach quiver with impending excitement. It was only the approaching holiday season bringing out this feeling in her, she immediately rationalized, shoving it aside and out of her mind.

She wasn't looking for love or romance, she told herself. Not now, anyway; not until this campaign was over. Not before she was properly prepared for it, she thought decidedly.

Hally was unprepared for what met her as she stepped through the door marked simply: GOURMET HEARTS. It wasn't as if the long, curving corridors she'd strode through were brightly lit, or that the decor of the lodge didn't reek of ambience—with deer antlers branching out at her from every corner, and glowering-eyed mounted bear heads following her accusingly as she strode past. But she'd half expected, at least, a classroom kind of atmosphere—with desks, perhaps, and fluorescent ceiling lights.

What she found, however, made her pause in the doorway. She blinked back at the eleven strange faces gazing up at her from the nondescript sofas and couches. The lighting was dimmed, falling about the room with a slightly reddish tint that seemed to soften everyone's features. A faint aroma of cinnamon and cloves wafted in the air—or was it nutmeg? Hally couldn't rightly tell. But her eyes were drawn instinctively to the far end of the room where a rotund man stood bathed in bright light. A chef's hat sat poised on the man's great head, the ears jutting out like open hands waving hello.

Hally glanced at her watch. She hated being late. Only twice in the eleven years she'd worked at Necessitas had she ever come into the office late—though she was the type of person who preferred being early, rather than just on time. And so her sudden embarassment came not from the stares of the other students, but from the fact that she was three and a half minutes late.

"I'm sorry I'm la—" Something snagged at her foot, and before she could discern the obstacle, she went sprawling helplessly forward.

Arms caught her before she hit the floor.

"Oopsy daisy," the voice said in a deep singsong voice.

Hally stared into the grinning face, her eyes meeting for a brief moment the man's amused gaze. His soft brown eyes watched her, narrowed, then blinked as if in sudden recognition. Hally felt the heat rush to her face, and she quickly righted herself, looking away.

"Thanks," she muttered, then noted with increasing embarrassment the splayed contents of her briefcase. Why hadn't she gotten that stupid clasp fixed?

As she bent down to scoop up her workfiles, the man knelt before her and picked up last month's issue of *Life Worth Living* magazine. He turned it over in his hands.

"Hmmm ... 'America's Most Eligible Bachelors,'" he read to himself. He glanced up at her, his grin widening. "Some light reading?"

"Research," Hally found herself muttering. The research department had dropped it off just before she'd left work.

"Mind if I borrow this?" he asked, flipping open the cover.

"I haven't read it yet—"

"Need some help here?" Another man with slicked-back hair and startlingly chiseled features retrieved a rolling pen. He handed it to Hally, his smile leering and

The Gourmet Cupid 27

flirtatious. Hally was aware of the others in the room staring at her. Her clumsy entrance, she realized with chagrin, had for the moment moved the spotlight from the man in the chef's hat to her.

Hally managed a self-possessed smile and stood, straightening her skirt and running her fingers down the buttons of her suit jacket. A blond tendril fell loose from her French braid and dangled against the hollow of her cheek.

The man with the slicked-back hair touched her arm. "Are you all right, Miss?"

"Ah! Miss Chrisswell! It is a pleasure to have you with us," the man in the chef's hat greeted her with uplifted arms. "Finally, all my Gourmet Hearts are assembled. Please, take your seat." He gestured to the empty space on the couch next to another man with thick spectacles and thinning, almost colorless hair.

"I'm Michael." The man with the slicked-back hair held out his hand.

"Hi. Hally Chrisswell." She shook his hand, and felt his fingers linger for a moment in her palm.

There was something almost catlike, she thought, in this man's mannerisms. Hally glanced over at the other man, who was still flipping through her borrowed copy of *Life Worth Living*.

"Uh, excuse me." She cocked an eyebrow at him.

"Oh, yeah. Here." He handed her the magazine.

Hally noted the youthful, pouty lips, the slight puffiness about the eyes which made her think back to her old college days—late nights fired by caffeine and doughnuts studying for art history and English finals in her dormitory. But she gathered this man was older than he appeared, despite the jeans and casual sweater, which, she did not fail to observe, were of an expensive quality.

"That's some research you're doing," he said, still holding out the magazine. "But meeting the right person can be tough. I like your strategy: check out his credit rating first, then go for the jugular. After all, a peek at the wallet in time saves nine.''

''I am not looking for a hus—'' She suddenly cut herself off and snatched the magazine from his grasp.

Why was she bothering to explain herself? She shoved the research department's copy of *Life Worth Living* back into her briefcase, but much to her dismay she could feel her face beginning to grow hot under his curious gaze.

As she made her way to the couch, she made a conscious effort to compose herself. Did she know this man? she found herself wondering, for in that brief instant when their eyes had met she'd not failed to notice his startled expression—almost a look of real recognition. But no, she could not place the face.

''For those who don't already know me,'' the big man in the chef's hat was saying, ''I am Lou Jay, Chef Gourmet!'' He flourished an invisible signature in the air and bowed as everyone applauded uncertainly.

A card with her name on it had been placed next to the man with the thinning hair, and Hally saw the man wore rimless spectacles that dilated his blue eyes to the size of quarters. She sat down and smiled at him. Immediately his face flushed scarlet, and the luminous eyes behind the thick lenses drifted to his hands entwined nervously in his lap.

''Everyone turn to your left and say hello to their cooking partners,'' said Lou Jay. ''This person will be your 'Gourmet Heart' for the remainder of these classes.''

The couch sank to her left, and Hally's knees swayed with the motion, brushing against the legs of the man with the penetrating light brown eyes. She quelled a moan as he leaned toward her, whispering: ''Hello, partner.'' He offered her his hand. ''Name's Ben.''

Hally nodded mutely and gave his hand a brief shake. Already she was noting, with alarm and dismay, a strategy at play about the room. Six men, six women: all seated about the illumined kitchen like a well-planned dinner table: boy, girl, boy, girl . . .

Oh, wonderful. I've landed in the middle of "The Dating Game," she thought with a groan. She inwardly cursed Tina for getting her into this awkward situation.

Hally slowly returned her gaze to the man she'd met: her chosen "Gourmet Heart." His brows lifted and he grinned a grin that sparked a mischievous twinkle in his eyes, which Hally saw now were not, in fact, brown, but a dark green. She frowned; the lighting in the room was playing tricks, she thought.

"I'm Hal—" she began.

"Hally Chrisswell," he said, nodding, seeming to mull the name over in his mind for a moment. "We haven't met before, have we?" he asked, his brows drawing together.

Was she misreading his expression? Was that suspicion she'd just observed flitting across his face? But the room was shrouded in pale shadows, sprayed in light that softened and rounded edges, concealed cracks, flaws—hid the truth.

She gazed at him blankly. "Um, I don't think we've met," she said. "Ben—I'm sorry, I didn't catch your last name."

Hally thought she saw him hesitate, but for a split second. He chewed on his lower lip and smiled. "Atkinson—Ben Atkinson," he said. "You sure we don't know each other?"

Names blurred before her as she mentally shuffled through her files of client names. No, no Atkinsons. She tugged on her earlobe, trying to think. Had she perhaps met him at a business convention? But she didn't recognize his face at all. And then Hally thought about all the blind dates Tina had set her up with over the years. Uh-oh, had Tina once set her up with this man?

But no, she would have remembered this one, she immediately thought, stealing a glance at her cooking partner. This man had something different about him—

"I'm sorry," she said, shaking her head. "I don't remember ever meeting you."

The wariness suddenly left his face, and he sat back with a satisfied grin.

"We ready to begin then, my budding Gourmet Hearts?" Lou Jay clapped his hands, then rubbed the palms together.

Hally frowned. Despite her concerted efforts to remain focused on the course at hand, her curiosity was now ineffably piqued. She was sensing a mystery burgeoning up around this man, something that was instinctively drawing her to him.

Whoa! You are not here to get involved, Hally, she reminded herself. *You're here to learn how to cook.*

Lou Jay was juggling potatoes. "Potatoes, *pommes de terre, Kartoffeln*—apples of the ground. Is there anything so lovely as the potato?" he sang. And then suddenly he was tossing them at the group. "Ah, but you must see for yourself, eh?"

One potato landed somewhere at the other end of the room. Another one was tossed in Hally's direction, and Ben reached up and caught it just before it was about to plow into Hally's nose.

"Reflex." He grinned, holding up the potato. Hally rolled her eyes and fished out a notepad and a pen from her briefcase.

The third potato reached the middle of the group, and was fumbled by a slender, long-legged woman with a thick mane of auburn curls. Her partner, the man with the slicked-back hair, retrieved it and handed it back to her with a seductive, but ingratiating smile. She giggled,

The Gourmet Cupid

not unaware of the stares from the other males in the room.

Hally noticed Ben noticing the woman, and she harrumphed, loudly enough for him to hear. He raised his brows and gazed back at Hally inquiringly.

"Today, we focus on the eyes, yes? What we see is, after all, as important as what we taste, no?" Lou Jay gestured grandly, his thick arms moving like a performer, reveling in his own passion. "And much of the time what we do see is only what we expect to see, eh? Eh?"

Ben passed her the potato as she scribbled down notes. He peered over her shoulder and down at the notepad. " 'Hally is a conscientious and responsible student,' " he mimicked in a nasal voice. He harrumphed and smiled. "I bet all your teachers just adored you."

Hally shot him a sidelong look and studied the potato in her hand. It was just a potato; unwashed, bumpy, and dirty—a vegetable she'd actually been able to bake successfully in the microwave. Nothing new here. She passed it along to the man with the thick glasses and thinning hair. His face reddened as her fingers brushed his.

"My name is Charles, by the way," he sputtered. "Charles Radcliffe."

"Hally Chrisswell." She smiled.

"My sister enrolled me in this class," he said, as if in apology. "To—you know . . . meet people." And he blushed again.

Hally glanced over at his partner, a small mousy woman whose attention seemed to be fixated on her shoes. She wore spectacles as well, and her straight brown hair was tied back severely into a ponytail. Charles gingerly placed the potato in the woman's lap, and her eyes flicked up for an instant, then returned to her shoes as she half-tossed the potato into the hands of the next man.

"Hot Potato," murmured Ben.

Lou Jay continued to expound on color and texture—"vegetable topography," as he termed it—all the while throwing at them carrots, strawberries, blueberries, and asparagus. Hally scribbled furiously in her notepad. But soon she found herself juggling fruits and vegetables, including the original potatoes which were making their third way round the room.

In the meantime, Lou Jay was ticking off cooking adjectives, pacing back and forth behind the kitchen counter:

"... chopping, slicing, dicing, peeling, mashing, kneading, squeezing, grinding, grating..."

"I think you missed 'sautéeing' and 'simmering,'" Ben whispered in her ear.

Hally pursed her lips and ignored him.

Lou Jay stopped suddenly in midpace. And he turned, as if all of a sudden becoming aware of his audience. He leaned forward on the counter, propped up by arms Hally imagined could crack coconuts, and stared at his students. His fleshy round face was flushed with passion. Everyone ceased the produce-passing line, and gazed up at him expectantly.

"But before I go on, I must share with you, my fellow food lovers, the true secret of gourmet cooking."

Hally held her pen poised, waiting, listening intently.

"The true secret of gourmet cooking lies here." Lou Jay slapped his chest. "Here, in the heart."

Hally rolled her eyes, a groan escaping from her throat. She should have known this would be a waste of time.

"And now we will look at the mushroom." He tossed a mushroom to Ben, who had to shuffle a plum, an apricot, and a tomato into the other hand.

"Voilà the *morelle*," introduced Lou Jay. But his tone was sober, his ruddy face transforming into a mask of sudden seriousness. "While the mushroom has no nutritional value that we know of, it does lend the gourmet dish extraordinary depth, dimension . . . a raison d'être." His face lit up again. *"Morelle.* Say it with me, my fellow Gourmet Hearts."

I wish he'd cut out that "Gourmet Heart" stuff and get down to business, Hally grumbled silently. But she wrote it down in her notepad and underlined it twice.

"Morelle," she heard Ben chant with the rest of the group. "Come on, Hally." He nudged her with his shoulder. "Get with the program. We don't need any sour grapes mushrooming in this class." He laughed at his own joke, oblivious to Hally's black look.

Another mushroom was tossed to the opposite end just as Ben placed the *morelle* upon Hally's notebook. Hally picked it up and Ben passed over the plum and apricot. She let out a breath of frustration through gritted teeth.

"Chanterelle!" expounded Lou Jay, his excitement mounting.

Another mushroom arced through the air, and Michael, the man with the slicked-back hair, reached over and caught it as his pretty partner in the short black dress recoiled. She looked over at him with that expression Hally had often seen on faces of women who flirted openly—who know how to get what they wanted, who know how to play "the game." Hally herself was unable to play that particular game; flirting was something that did not come naturally with her. Perhaps if she'd exerted herself, put in as much effort into a relationship as she did in her job—

"Shiitake!"

Another mushroom flew into the air, and like a group of backup singers, Hally and the other Gourmet Hearts melodically echoed the name.

The strawberry was by this time bruised and battered, its red flesh beginning to leave red stains on the hands that passed it along, and when Ben dropped it into her palm, Hally let it slip through her fingers. A curse slid off her tongue before she could reign it in.

"Oops. Sorry." Ben immediately produced a handkerchief and daubed at the stain on her skirt. Hally felt the warmth of his hand through the linen material, and something in her lurched, sounding off a siren inside her.

"Thank you," she said, snatching the handkerchief out of his hand, "but I think I can handle this on my own." She glanced at the initials embroidered into the corner: *B. A.* And she swore under her breath as the strawberry stain only deepened, seeming now to have entrenched itself in the fabric.

"This was a three-hundred-dollar suit," she wailed furiously.

"I'm sure you've got three or four suits just like it hanging in your closet," said Ben, his eyebrows quirking up.

He was gazing at her, taking in her flaxen hair woven tightly into a French braid, the classic, streamlined cut of her gray suit, the polished patent leather pumps. Everything about Hally—except for the single tendril of hair which she'd hastily twirled back behind her ear, and now the coin-sized red stain in the lap of her skirt—was perfect, immaculate.

"You look like you need to let your hair down— loosen some of those bolts that've got you so . . . uptight," said Ben, imitating the closed, rigid way she was sitting, his spine straightening to exaggeration.

"I'm not uptight," she countered defensively.

"Uh-huh," he said sardonically. "I'm betting you're an attorney, maybe a criminal prosecuting lawyer—"

"For your information—"

"No, wait. Let me guess. I'm good at these kinds of things—reading people, I mean." He cupped his chin thoughtfully, regarding her with a kittenish grin. "I've got it. You're an executive of some sort. Lessee... accounting? No..."

"I'm in advertising," Hally cut in with an impatient sigh. But she immediately regretted this admission of information; she'd not wanted to reveal too much about herself, not get too personally involved—especially with this man.

"Advertising, huh? What firm do you—"

"Everyone into the kitchen! Chop chop! There is work to be done!" Lou Jay clapped his hands, summoning them toward the fluorescent-lit kitchen.

"Finally," grumbled Hally, leaping to her feet. Now maybe they could actually start in on what she'd signed up for in the first place. She tucked her notebook and pen under her arm and followed the others into the kitchen.

She selected an apron from the counter and tied it around her waist. Mozart floated into the room as Lou Jay pulled out vats of potatoes, strawberries and blueberries, tomatoes, mushrooms, and a basket of garlic bulbs.

"Ah, garlic. An aphrodisiac to be sure—and an ingredient of vast importance in gourmet cooking," Lou Jay informed them, holding up a garlic bulb. He brought it to his nose and sniffed deeply. "Oh, I see the worry on your faces. You are worrying about bad breath." He gave a snorting laugh. "But believe me, a properly prepared and baked clove, delicious and tantalizing though it may be, will—contrary to popular belief—will not advertise itself after the meal."

"Now, there's a snappy campaign slogan for you," Ben whispered in her ear. 'Garlic: the aphrodisiac that won't advertise itself after a romantic meal.' "

Hally flicked an annoyed sideways glance at him. Again she chastised herself for letting him goad her into revealing what she did for a living. She glanced over at the others, noting the shy and flirtatious smiles, a bright, fervent eagerness glittering in their eyes. This cooking course, she realized with a silent groan, was for them but a culinary expressway to love—Charles was enough evidence of that. These Gourmet Hearts were not so much interested in cooking up a gourmet meal as they were in cooking up a romantic relationship.

As Lou Jay demonstrated the peeling of the single garlic clove, whacking it gently with the side of an enormous butcherlike blade, Hally scribbled in her notepad. She made a small note at the top about the knife; at home her cutlery drawer consisted of one dulled, two-inch blade, which she used to do everything from slicing an apple to hewing tough defrosted roast beef slices warmed up in the microwave.

It soon became apparent, as Lou Jay gave them the tour of the kitchen, that these bushels and colanders and vats of produce were not present simply to serve as visual aids, but that they were to be active ingredients in tonight's gourmet lesson. Their teacher, with coconut-cracking arms a-flailing, demonstated how to destem and clean the strawberries and blueberries without squishing them, how to scrub potatoes, peel carrots and asparagus stalks. He paused for a moment when he came to the mushrooms.

"Now, when it comes to the mushroom, this rule always, always applies," said Lou Jay, the sound of violins humming like eavesdropping mosquitos in the background. Hally wrote "MUSHROOMS" in large capital letters, and asterisked it.

Ben glanced over her shoulder, and Hally shifted so he couldn't look at what she was writing.

"You're not writing something about me, are you?" He cocked an amused eyebrow.

"Don't flatter yourself," she mumbled.

"Never—never, never, never, wash mushrooms in water," said Lou Jay, shaking his head.

"Why not?" Michael's partner asked. She tossed back her long auburn curls, running her hands along the hips of her short black dress. In the fluorescent light, Hally could see she was older than she initially guessed, maybe in her late thirties—five or six years older than Hally. But she was definitely attractive, and six pairs of male eyes instantly turned to her, riveted. Hally snuck a quick glance over at Ben, whose mouth gaped slightly.

Disgust and irritation—and something else—nudged its way into her chest. She ran her tongue over her teeth, the muscle in her jaw twitching.

Michael, smoothing back his slicked-back hair, caught her look and winked. Hally looked away, pretending to be absorbed by Lou Jay's rambling explanation. She'd given up trying to scribble everything down in her small notebook, but she did notice one man standing slightly outside the group watching her intently. No, it wasn't her he was watching, but Ben.

In his hand he held a mini–tape recorder. He wore a pale yellow shirt and jeans, and for an instant, Hally thought she recognized him.

Lou Jay was organizing them, and Hally and Ben found themselves being delegated to a pailful of potatoes.

"We're washing potatoes?" she said, incredulous.

Ben rolled up his sleeves, shrugging. He picked up the two soft-bristled brushes and handed her one.

"Well, all's fair in food and war. You have to start somewhere, I suppose." He grinned, dumping handfuls of potatoes in the sink. "Shall we, partner? Or are you afraid to get your hands dirty?"

Hally wrinkled her nose and tugged at her earlobe. Lou Jay pranced behind them, humming with the music. "Ah . . . Music and food and love. Is this not the life, eh? Open your hearts and let Mozart guide you into the romantic world of food.''

There's nothing romantic about scrubbing potatoes, Hally grumbled silently. She glanced over at the others who were already delving, with a little uncertainty and trepidation, into their appointed tasks. However, the music seemed to be having a relaxing effect on the group as tensions slowly dispelled and a friendly murmuring rose up around them.

But out of the corner of her eye, Hally saw the man with the minirecorder making his way toward them.

"Excuse me," he said, tapping Ben on the shoulder. "But aren't you—"

"Ben Atkinson," said Hally's partner before the man could finish. Ben withdrew his wet hand from the sink and shook the man's hand heartily.

The man looked at his hand and wiped it on his apron. "Oh, I'm sorry. I thought you were someone else," he said, staring now. "But the similarity is uncanny. For a moment I thought you were—"

"This is Hally Chrisswell." Ben gestured to Hally with his head. "She's in advertising."

Hally bit her lip and strained out a polite smile.

"Karl MacAvoy." The man nodded, shaking her hand. But his attention was still on Ben. "Well, you probably get this all the time—being mistaken for B—"

"I just have that kind of face, I guess," said Ben quickly, and he laughed.

Suddenly, Hally remembered where she'd seen this man before. "You're that restaurant critic," she said. "From 'Milwaukee's Dining Room.' "

"Yes. Actually, I like to think of myself as a journalist." He glanced at Ben who had returned to his scrubbing. "I'm doing a piece on cooking classes—"

"Tsk, tsk, Mr. MacAvoy. You won't learn how to peel

asparagus chatting with your classmates, now will you?" Lou Jay put his hand on the man's shoulder.

"But, I just—"

"Now, now. Don't worry. Your turn to clean potatoes will come." And he guided the journalist back to the other end of the kitchen.

Hally screwed up her face, regarding the pail of potatoes doubtfully. "I thought we were going to learn how to cook."

Ben eyed her. "Hardly the kind of work for an advertising executive."

"I'm not an—" *Advertising executive*, she was about to say. But she stopped herself; after all, he didn't have to know she was only an art director, appointed as the advertising executive for her team by default. No, the less this man knew about her, the better.

"Not afraid of a little hard work, are you?" he goaded, his green eyes twinkling.

Hally compressed her lips stubbornly, and rolled up her sleeves. No one had ever accused her of being afraid of hard work—even if it entailed washing vegetables. She plunged her hands into the water, extracted a potato, and began to scrub.

"Whoa! Leave some for the others." Ben grinned, watching her. "Are you always this aggressive? You must be a real dynamo at—what company did you say you worked for?"

"I didn't."

"Oh, is it a secret, then? Is it a disreputable firm? Or is it that you're ashamed of what you do?"

"Ashamed? No, of course I'm not ashamed of my job," retorted Hally indignantly.

"Hmm... I wouldn't have pegged you as the advertising executive type. You... you don't have the face for it, for one."

"What do you mean, I don't have the 'face for it'?" she asked, vexed.

"Well, isn't advertising just a professional form of lying?" said Ben.

"Obviously, you don't know anything about the advertising business," retorted Hally.

Ben's green eyes twinkled. He cocked an eyebrow. "Well, maybe you could teach me—educate me on the finer points of advertising. And"—he smiled demurely—"as it so happens, I'm free later this evening."

"Well, I'm not."

"Oh? Hot date?"

"No, I have to work."

"Tomorrow night, then."

"I can't—"

Ben let out a snort. "Don't tell me. You have to work."

"No," said Hally with a small smile. "I have a hot date."

"Oh, so you do actually have a life outside work. I figured you for the stay-at-home-with-the-cat kind of girl. Someone who watches *Breakfast at Tiffany's* every weekend and secretly wishes she could be more like Holly Golightly."

"Hah! Shows how little you do know about me," said Hally triumphantly. "I don't have a cat." Though *Breakfast at Tiffany's* was one of her favorite films.

Just as Ben was about to respond, Lou Jay clapped his big hands and directed everyone to switch tasks with the partners to their right. Hally smiled at Charles, who flushed and glanced over at his mousy cooking partner. The woman smiled shyly up at him.

My goodness, thought Hally. *These two are already becoming smitten with each other.*

She stared at the mound of carrot peelings, and the even bigger pile of carrots, and let out a long sigh. She had a ton of important work waiting for her at home, and here she was washing potatoes and peeling carrots.

"So." Ben picked up the carrot peeler. "What are you working on now? Some prestigious computer company? A new brand of washing detergent? Or maybe some gourmet product—" He looked suddenly thoughtful. "Which would make sense, you enrolling in this course—"

"So, what do you do, Mr. Atkinson?" Hally swiftly cut in, steering the conversation away from herself.

"Ben. Please call me Ben. Since we're going to be cooking partners—Gourmet Hearts," he amended, "I think we might as well address each other by our first names, don't you think?"

"Okay . . . Ben." She began peeling. "What is it that you do?"

He shrugged. "I do a lot of things."

"Such as . . . ?"

"I guess you could say that I, well, that I'm following in my father's footsteps."

"And what does your father do?"

"He owns his own company."

Hally frowned, giving him a sidelong glance. It seemed strange to her that this man wasn't forthcoming with personal information. Most men she knew liked to rattle off their résumé the moment she met them. Was he trying to hide something?

"Dare I ask the name of your father's company?"

Ben's green eyes gazed levelly into hers. "You first."

They stared at each other for a long moment until Hally dropped her gaze. Her heart, she noted with dismay, was beating hard and fast.

"Okay. Stalemate. Let's, uh—" Hally moistened her lips. "Let's just stick to the cooking, shall we?"

"Hmm . . . I'm already cooking," murmured Ben.

And Hally pretended not to hear this, but his words

caused a slow flush to rise to her cheeks, anyway. She forced herself not to read any subtle meaning in his response, and struggled to ignore the faint rise of pleasure and excitement they stirred in her.

Later that evening, when she finally gave up on the mockups for the Nobler Kitty Litter account, Hally dragged herself off to bed. She was irritated by her distraction, her thoughts seeming to unravel the more she tried to concentrate on her work.

She rubbed the small of her back as she slipped in between the covers. The smell of garlic still lingered on her fingers, even after twenty minutes of scrubbing in the bath.

"Won't advertise on you the next day, huh? Yeah, that's fine if you're *eating* baked garlic." She scowled, and gazed at her wrinkled, flaky hands. She reached for the magnolia lotion on her bedside table.

As she massaged in the lotion—for the third time—her thoughts began to meander again. She didn't know why, but there was something about that man, Ben Atkinson, that bothered her. She couldn't shrug off this feeling that she should know him from somewhere. And she knew now that he was hiding something. But what?

But was there really a mystery surrounding this Ben Atkinson—or was she reading too much into this? Creating a mystery where there was none?

Aagh! She didn't have time for this! She needed to keep her thoughts focused. The Nobler Kitty Litter account was due next week, and Wade had asked her to meet with the clients of Milwaukee Scents on Wednesday. Marla's wedding was in two weeks, and Danny had said something about his son's hockey tournament being the week of the Bel Abner presentation.

And then there was Thanksgiving.

This year, Hally had opted not to take vacation days.

Her parents were still on their world cruise, and her brother and his family were spending the holidays in Bermuda.

Thanksgiving and Christmas day would not be spent alone, however. Tina had invited her again, as she did every year, and naturally, her friend had, in her characteristic subtle fashion, extended the invitation to include a "date."

"Hey, you never know, Hally. By Thanksgiving, you might have found someone . . . special." She'd said this the day before Serina Heineault had appointed her advertising executive of the Bel Abner account.

Someone special, hah! Fat chance; she had enough on her plate now, as it was. She turned off the light and lay her head back against the pillow, yawning. She sniffed her hands. Yecch! Magnolia-scented garlic. It was almost as if the garlic had seeped into her body and was floating in her bloodstream. "An aphrodisiac," Lou Jay had called it.

"Aphrodisiac, my foot," grumbled Hally. She closed her eyes and turned on her side, shutting out all thoughts of Lou Jay and his bizarre gourmet class.

But, nonetheless, into her dreams came waltzing a parade of potatoes and asparagus and strawberries. Carrots and blueberries and tiny cloves of garlic swayed together in time to the soft romantic sounds of Mozart.

And then, Ben Atkinson was suddenly there, grinning and watching her with those penetrating green eyes of his. He reached for her hand and swept her into the kitchen, and under the fluorescent lights they danced with the vegetables and fruit.

Chapter Three

"Why do you keep smelling your fingers?" Tina lifted the cellophane off the trifle. "For a while there, I thought you were trying to signal me." Tina sighed. "I kept thinking, 'Do I stink?' I smelled Garry; he's fine. Roger might have on a little too much Polo—"

"No, it's my hands. Go ahead. Smell." Hally held her hand up to Tina's nose.

"What? They smell like...I don't know, magnolias?"

"Garlic," grumbled Hally. "You don't think they smell like garlic?"

Tina shot her friend a hard look. "No. I don't think they smell like garlic. Gee, what's wrong with you? You hardly said a word all evening." She arranged four teacups on a tray, and reached for the coffeepot. "What's got you so distracted, anyway?"

Hally winced and kneaded the muscle between her shoulders. "It's that stupid cooking class."

"Oh, right." Tina scrutinized her trifle critically. "How'd that go, anyway?" She poked the dessert, grimacing. "Maybe I should have enrolled in that class with you."

"Hmm...if you like working in a scullery." Hally let out a groan. "I'm paying this guy to let me scrub potatoes and peel carrots."

"Does the trifle look a little flat to you?" Tina frowned. "So did you meet anyone...interesting?"

"Interesting? Huh, well, interesting, yes—but *exasperating* might be a better word to describe him." Not to mention "arrogant"—and "mysterious," she added silently. Hally thought about Ben Atkinson, and felt a peculiar tug in her chest.

Tina regarded her with raised brows. "Him? You mean the gourmet chef, Lou Jay?"

"No," sighed Hally, "my cooking partner, Ben Atkinson. He's . . . he—" She faltered for a moment, struggling to find the right words to describe him. She realized she was unable to put her finger on what exactly it was about Ben Atkinson that managed to stir in her this strange reaction.

"Well, this *is* interesting." Tina grinned. "What does this Ben Atkinson do for a living?"

"I don't know."

"You don't know?"

"No, he's kind of, well—secretive."

A look of understanding suddenly crossed Tina's face. "Aha. I see now why you're attracted to this guy."

"I'm not attracted to him! He's just so—" Hally threw up her hands in exasperation. "I don't know."

"Is he good-looking?"

"Tina! Looks have nothing to do with it."

"So you are attracted to this Ben Atkinson."

"I didn't say that—"

Garry poked his head in. "How're you doing in here, girls? Listen, Roger was just suggesting we go out for dessert. He knows this place in Brookfield—" He glanced at the coffee and the trifle on the counter. "Oh, but I guess we have dessert already covered."

Tina grimaced and nudged the trifle, which had now begun to cave in at the middle. "Actually, that sounds great."

Hally consulted her watch. "It's getting late, and I still have some work I have to—"

"Aw, come on, Hally." Tina put her arm around her friend. "Take a night off, just this once. It'll be good for you to get out. Live a little." She patted her short curls, and sighed. "Besides, I've been cooped up in this kitchen all day."

"But I—"

"Hally, did you know Roger went to Harvard? Garry says he's one of the best agents in the company. Smart— and handsome, too. Don't you think?" Tina led her out of the kitchen. "He may not be as secretive as your Ben Atkinson," she whispered, "but he's a career man, and I know for a fact that he's looking for someone just like you. You two are perfect for each other."

How many times had she heard Tina tell her this? thought Hally as she strode into the living room.

Immediately upon seeing her, Roger's face lit up and he rose from the couch.

"Okay, we're game," Tina addressed Roger. "How do you want to do this?" And without waiting for a response she said, "Well, since Hally didn't bring her car, I guess Garry and I will follow you two in yours."

Hally's nostrils flared slightly. She should have suspected an ulterior motive when Tina had offered to come pick her up at her apartment.

"Yes, that sounds like a plan—that is, if it's all right with you, Hally." Roger turned to her, straightening his silk tie.

"Oh, uh, yes. That's fine," she answered.

As they moved into the hall, Hally cast her friend a black look. But Tina only returned it with a triumphant smile.

Roger drove a BMW whose interior smelled of Polo and vanilla, and that overall pervasive odor of success. Hally glimpsed the Rolex on his wrist, and noted the London Fog trenchcoat that he donned over his gray Armani suit. His hair was clipped conservatively over

The Gourmet Cupid 47

his ears, styled to control the thick wave at the top. He held his shoulders squarely, his chin thrust out a little, lending to his profile a look of confidence and self-poise.

He did seem a perfect match for her, mused Hally.

Tonight, she'd pulled her blond hair into a simple twist and had pinned it up from her neck. She'd opted to wear her charcoal gray suit dress, which, she noted, matched his gray Armani suit quite nicely. Seeing the two of them together, no one would doubt that they were a perfect couple.

"I guess this is a kind of celebratory dinner for you, tonight, Hally," said Roger, smiling over at her.

Hally frowned. "Excuse me?"

"Your promotion. Garry was telling me you were just recently promoted to advertising executive."

Hally pursed her lips. "Hmm... well, not exactly. I've just been put in charge of a new campaign. I'm still officially just an art director."

"Just an art director? Well, that's nothing to sneer at," said Roger soberly. "I bet you're very good at your job. You work for Necessitas, isn't that right?"

"Yes." Hally brought her fingers to her nose, but all she could smell now was Roger's aftershave. "It's only a small advertising company."

"But reputable in its own right. Necessitas has a good standing in this city's business community," Roger reassured her. "For instance, your pension plans are one of the best..." And he went on to discuss retirement packages and insurance policies, expounding on details that wafted incomprehensibly over her head, leaving her to intermittently turn her head and nod as if she were taking it all in.

When they finally arrived at the restaurant, Roger was still explaining about fluctuating insurance rates, and probability rates. Hally's face felt sore from smiling and trying to fight back a yawn.

"My goodness!" exclaimed Tina as they strode up the cobblestone walkway to the restaurant. She glanced back at the black stretch limousine and patted her curls. "I hope we're dressed for this place!"

"It's one of my favorite places to take clients," said Roger, pleased. "They have a chocolate mousse here that is absolutely heavenly. The chef here is supposed to be one of the best gourmet cooks in Wisconsin."

"Well, what a coincidence. Hally, here, is taking a gourmet—Ow!" She rubbed her arm where Hally had pinched it.

"I hope no one here is trying to watch their weight." Roger flashed them a grin. "You pay an arm and a leg here, but the desserts are definitely worth it."

"Oh, Hally can eat and eat—and she never seems to put on weight," said Tina, eyeing her friend. "Me, on the other hand—"

"With you being such an incredible cook, Tina, it's a wonder you're so nice and slim," said Roger.

Tina beamed. She grinned at Hally and waggled her brows, her expression seeming to say: "See? I told you he was perfect for you." Hally yawned behind Roger's back.

The restaurant was crowded, but the maître d', appearing to recognize Roger after they shook hands, promptly seated the four of them. Hally took in the expensive and flashy vestiture of the customers, the younger women dressed in low-cut evening gowns, smoking and looking bored. The place reeked of old money, with new business deals being made over champagne and cappuccinos in an indulgent fog of cigar smoke.

Hally gazed admiringly at the shiny mahogany tabletops, observing the gallery of prints and paintings that decorated the walls. The miniature Tiffany lamps shed a quaint, intimate light over the tables, the resulting atmosphere reminding Hally of one of those elegant European bistros she'd seen in decorating magazines.

Roger leaned over and put his hand on hers. "How about some champagne to celebrate your new campaign?"

Hally declined, and smiled politely. "Just coffee for me, thanks." And as she said this, she noticed a man getting up from a table at the far end of the restaurant.

Her eyes followed him as he crossed to the entrance, buttoning his jacket, laughing and nodding his head at the tall, lithe-bodied woman beside him. The woman wore a silver sequined dress, the plunging neckline accentuating her figure. Her deep chestnut brown hair glowed luxuriously in the restaurant light. Her date put his hand on her narrow waist and walked her to the door. As his head turned vaguely toward Hally, she gave a short gasp.

Hally ducked, her heart pounding against her ribs as she pretended to adjust something on her shoe.

"Hally? You okay?" Tina tilted her head, watching her with bemusement.

"Yes, uh, just fixing my shoe." She raised her head in time to see Ben Atkinson and the woman in the silver dress move toward the exit.

"Someone you know?" frowned Roger, following her gaze.

Hally quickly averted her eyes. "Someone I know? No." Which wasn't a lie in itself; what did she really know about Ben Atkinson?

"Hey! Wasn't that Veronica Wilmott?" said Garry, gazing at the entrance.

"You mean the television actress? Where?" Tina whirled around excitedly to where her husband was still gazing. But they'd already left. "Darn, I must have just missed her."

"Who was that man with her? He looked familiar," said Roger.

Ben Atkinson, answered Hally silently. But what was he doing with Veronica Wilmott? Was he an agent? A television director? An actor? No, not an actor; she was sure she would have recognized him before.

Hmm . . . , she thought primly. He certainly had nerve. Only yesterday he'd asked her out, and here he was at an expensive restaurant, dating a television actress. Well, now she certainly had no illusions of what kind of man this Ben Atkinson was. Certainly not a one-woman man, she thought. And she supposed, for someone like Ben Atkinson, Lou Jay's gourmet class was perfect, which was, in effect, "The Love Connection" masquerading as a cooking class.

"Hally? What do you think?" Roger and Garry and Tina stared at her expectantly.

"Well . . . uh, yes, sure."

Tina's mouth opened, and Garry gazed at her bemusedly. Roger frowned, then suddenly let out a low laugh.

"Oh, I see. Ha-ha! That's funny." Roger chuckled. "Tina didn't tell me about your sense of humor. You're a riot, Hally," and they all laughed, Hally a little uncertainly.

Hally smiled, confused. *Yes, I'm a riot, all right,* she thought, trying to focus on the conversation.

But she glanced back at the restaurant entrance uneasily, wondering if Ben Atkinson had seen her—wondering why seeing him with that other woman bothered her so much.

Later, in the bathroom, Tina shook her head. "Hally, where are you? Tonight you agreed that it was a good idea to raise interest rates and abolish workers' compensation. And since when have you been against national health care? You're starting to sound like a right-wing conservative."

Hally stared at her reflection. "I—I have a lot on my mind, Tina. I have an account due this week." She sighed. "And then there's the Bel Abner campaign, and this . . . cooking course." She smelled her fingers. "I have a feeling that I'm going to have to teach myself how to cook up a gourmet meal."

"Hey, give it time, Hally. You've only had one class. Give it some time," Tina gazed at her friend's reflection, concerned. "You better slow down, Hal. You're still young; you don't want to burn out before you're—"

"I know, I know," said Hally, rubbing her neck. "Quit worrying, Tina. I'm not heading for a burnout. I can handle work."

"But you can't handle a relationship." Tina waved her hand to allay Hally's retort. "Yes, yes. I know, I know—you don't have to tell me." She smiled. "But Roger is a career man himself, and he respects you. He's just like you, in fact. Garry says he works twice as hard as any man in the company."

Hally said nothing. She was thinking about Ben Atkinson. Why did he have to show up tonight? But more to the point, why did she care?

"Like I said, he's perfect for you." Tina grinned.

As Hally emerged from the meeting room, she ran into Serina Heineault.

"Hello, Hally. How is the Bel Abner campaign shaping up?" She shifted her briefcase to the other hand. "I heard Prentice & Dreyer sent a representative to Venice."

Uh-oh. Don't tell me you're sending me to Venice.

However, there was a triumphant glint in Serina's dark eyes, and her red lipsticked mouth curved into a knowing smile. "If there's one thing I know about Deliah Abner, she is extremely protective of her privacy. And Randall Abner is equally protective of his wife."

She gave Hally's arm a reassuring pat. "I think your idea about the gourmet meal was brilliant, dear. It just may snag us this account, after all."

My idea? "Uh, Mrs. Heineault—"

"Serina. Well, keep up the good work, Hally." And she moved off down the hall, her briefcase swinging with an energetic momentum at her side, trying to keep up with her swift stride.

Hally made her way up to the research department.

"I'm looking for last month's *Life Worth Living*." She showed the man at the desk her card. "Uh, the issue that featured, uh, 'America's Most Eligible Bachelors'?"

The clerk regarded her over his bifocals, giving her a long look. "We only have hard copies of that particular magazine." And he disappeared into the archive room.

After only a few minutes, he returned. "All eight copies are signed out. One by you, I might add."

"Yes," said Hally, looking uncomfortable. "I seem to have misplaced my copy. Uh, can you tell me who has the other seven?"

"No, I'm sorry." The man frowned at the computer screen. "But I can tell you that no one else here in Necessitas signed them out. We do let certain clients and prospective clients use this facility, as well."

"But why would they want this issue of *Life Worth Living*?" said Hally, musing aloud.

The man shrugged, adjusted his bifocals, sat down, and returned to his computer.

Hally trudged wearily back to the elevator and returned to her office on the fourth floor. Nothing about this Bel Abner account seemed to be panning out for her.

She and Danny were still wrapped up in the Nobler Kitty Litter presentation, which looked, now, as though

The Gourmet Cupid 53

it wouldn't be ready for Friday. And Marla's attention was diverted by her impending wedding. They hadn't even started the Bel Abner campaign, and Hally found herself growing more irritable and distracted by the idea of this gourmet class. And she refused to believe that her cooking partner, Ben Atkinson, had anything to do with this sudden distraction, or that seeing him Saturday night with Veronica Wilmott had created this annoying creative block.

"Hally!" Marla was pulling on her coat, her face pink and pinched. "I have to take an early lunch. The dressmaker called; she's lost my measurements. Can you believe that?"

If the copywriter hadn't been near tears, Hally would have told her to put it off for later. But she simply nodded and smiled sympathetically and let her go.

Danny was nursing a coffee. He glanced up at Hally with bloodshot eyes, his nose swollen and red. "I dink I caught my son's coad." He sneezed.

"Great. Just don't get near me."

He hacked out a cough and moaned, pressing the palm of his hand to his forehead. He reached for a Kleenex and snuffled into it loudly.

Hally sighed. "Danny, why don't you go home, take care of that cold. I—I can hold the fort for now."

"Danks, Hally," sniffed Danny miserably. He collected his workboards and slid them into his case. Pinching his nose, he reached for his coat and turned to look at Hally. "You look tired, Hally. You sure you're okay?"

Hally forced a smile. "I'm fine. I can handle it."

Danny started for the door, then suddenly turned around, his brows drawn together in confusion. "Handle what?"

Okay, Hally, you can handle this, she told herself. She reluctantly pulled on the blindfold. "This is ridiculous."

"Trust me," said Ben.

Trust this man? she thought nervously.

"... when it comes to food preparation," Lou Jay was saying, "the nose is the head management. It must learn to distinguish smells—to discern which spice is working too hard or too little, which ingredient is absent, which herb needs help or is not doing its job."

"Are we going to cook a gourmet meal or make up a business brochure?" muttered Hally.

"... you must exercise the senses—stretch them as you would your own imagination. Revel in the aroma! Learn from your nose, my Gourmet Hearts. Allow the aroma of the herbs to imprint themselves on your memory."

Beethoven wafted in the background like a seamless, dramatic sea voyage in Hally's ears. Her head felt light and dizzy, and she clasped her hands together in her lap.

"Okay. Here's the first one," she heard Ben whisper. She could smell his aftershave cologne, a faintly floral but heady scent that reminded her of new-spring suede.

Feathery leaves suddenly tickled her upper lip, and she recoiled.

"Easy, now," he soothed, as if he were speaking to a wild, untethered mare. Hally straightened her back and took a deep breath.

"Uh, savory?" she guessed, sniffing.

"No, not savory."

Hally sniffed again, trying to remember the herbs they had passed back and forth earlier. "Fennel."

"Right. Now this one?"

She breathed in a lemony scent. "Lemon balm," she said right away.

"Yup." He held up another herb to her nose.

"Savory."

"No. Try again."

"Tarragon."

The Gourmet Cupid 55

"Nope."

"Uh, coriander?" This time she was guessing wildly.

Ben chuckled. "Good guess. How 'bout this one?"

"Savory."

"No." He laughed. "Smell it again." The leaves tickled her lips and chin. "You've got a very interesting nose, by the way."

Hally pursed her lips, frustrated by the heat that began to creep up to her cheeks. She could feel his eyes on her, grinning that annoyingly arrogant grin, enjoying her awkward position. Her hands went to her blindfold. But he stopped her.

"Uh-uh." He squeezed her hands gently. "Fair's fair. I did it; now you have to."

Hally steadied herself. Yes, he'd played out his turn without making one mistake. And, yes, she'd enjoyed being able to study him without those dark green eyes intruding. She visualized that strong chin, those soft pouty lips and slightly hooked nose as she drew in the scent of the herb.

"Chervil," she said finally.

"Good. And—?"

"Parsley."

"No."

"Tarragon."

"No."

Hally exhaled in frustration. "Savory?"

"Yes!"

"This is stupid."

"You don't do much cooking, do you? Okay, smell."

"Parsley," Hally said from out of left field. She scratched her nose.

"Uh-huh. See? You're getting the hang of this." But Hally detected the teasing lilt in Ben's voice. "Here. Try this."

"Dill," she sputtered as the tiny hairlike leaves tickled her lips. She suppressed an urge to bat at his hand. He changed herbs. She sniffed. "Tarragon. Is that it? Can I take this stupid thing—"

Ben caught her hand and laced his fingers in hers. She flushed and yanked her hand out of his grip.

"All right. Last, but not least," said Ben, holding the herb under her nose.

Hally mentally went through the previous names, inhaling the scent of the herb. "Um, lessee . . ."

"Process of elimination," harrumphed Ben. "I'll give you a hint. The Greeks used it as a symbol for cupidity—you know, being suddenly struck by the arrow of love—"

"Cumin," she said gruffly, cutting him off.

Hally wrenched off the blindfold, and in so doing, loosened some tendrils of blond hair. She quickly smoothed them back into place, blinking. Ben watched her, his expression strangely demure.

"You should wear your hair down. I bet you look great just before you go to bed—all that pent-up tension and tightness gone," he said, tilting his head.

"Thanks for the fashion tip, Mr. Coco Chanel," she said tartly. "Is this the kind of advice you give to the television stars you work with?"

Ben frowned. "Television?" And then he laughed. "What makes you think I work in television?"

"Oh, sorry. I meant the television stars you *date*," Hally amended.

"I've never dated a—" Sudden illumination crossed Ben's face. "Oh, you mean—"

"Look," she interrupted him, "I don't need to hear about your personal life. What you do on your own time is your business."

Ben looked at her, his eyebrows raising queryingly. The corners of his mouth turned up in a bemused, lopsided grin.

The Gourmet Cupid 57

Hally turned her head, hoping that the color of her face wasn't reflecting the fire of embarrassment that was flaming through her veins. It was the look he gave her—that taunting, teasing expression that seemed to spear right through her. The intensity of his gaze made her feel suddenly transparent, feeling almost as if he were burrowing into the chambers and pathways of her heart, reading the truth of her thoughts.

Not fair, she thought; she couldn't tell, let alone imagine, what he was thinking. He seemed to be a lot better at guarding his emotions.

She glanced over at Charles and his partner, who were still engaged in the smelling exercise. They sat very close to each other, their knees touching, giggling. The woman's face flushed suddenly, and Hally noticed Charles stroking her small white hand.

"Hmm... those two seem to be getting along, all right," said Ben in a low voice.

Karl MacAvoy peered over at them from the other end of the room. "That journalist seems awfully interested in you," she said, gesturing with her head. "Now, who is it, I wonder, he thinks he's mistaken you for?"

Ben immediately withdrew his grin, his expression turning inward. "How do you know it's me he's really interested in? And he's not the only one who's been trying to get your attention."

Hally followed Ben's gaze, and caught the eye of Michael, who raked his fingers through his slicked-back hair and winked. She smiled a polite smile in return, and immediately feigned sudden absorption in her briefcase, which she pulled in closer to her legs.

When everyone was finished with the "Aroma Knows Game"—as Lou Jay referred to it—the chef beckoned them to the kitchen.

"Now, I will show you how to create your own bouquets garnis," he announced.

"My mother always says, 'you're not a cook until you know what a bouquet garni is,' " said Ben.

"What is a bouquet garni?" she asked.

Ben shrugged. "How should I know; I'm not a cook yet."

Hally opened her notebook. "So your mother is a good cook?"

"She's almost as deft in the kitchen as my father."

"Ah, so you come from a family of cooks. Your father's business—"

"He inherited it, actually," said Ben quickly. "Oh, but that's boring stuff. Now, advertising—that's something worth talking about. You work for Prentice & Dreyer, isn't that right?"

Hally shot him a look of disgust. "I wouldn't be caught dead working for those unethical piranhas."

"No?" He frowned, but his green eyes were twinkling impishly. "I thought Prentice & Dreyer was supposed to be the most prestigious advertising company in Milwaukee."

Hally snorted loudly. "Who told you that?"

"Well . . . Prentice & Dreyer, actually."

"Hah! Necessitas has more prestige in its little finger than—" She stopped short, realizing her mistake.

"Ah, yes. Necessitas. I have heard of that company: 'the mother who lords over the destinies of men.' Isn't that Necessitas?"

"Actually, she's the *goddess* who presides over the destinies of *mankind*," corrected Hally. "And the *mother* of the Three Fates."

"Catchy." Ben grinned. "So you are a Necessitas goddess. Yes, it figures." His eyes moved down her body appraisingly.

Hally stiffened, her jaw muscles tightening. She wasn't going to give him the satisfaction of her embarrassment.

"Today we will be making fish bouquets garnis, yes?" Lou Jay was saying. Beethhoven responded with a hard cello downbeat. Hally began writing furiously in her notepad.

"One sprig of French tarragon—aaah, such a rapturous aroma, no? One sprig of fennel, two leaves of lemon balm—mmmm . . . so refreshing." Lou Jay sighed and tilted his face toward the ceiling. He closed his eyes and smiled. "Ah! It lifts the mood, soars us up into the heavens." He opened his eyes and regarded his students. "And we are all in happy, loving moods, are we not, my Gourmet Hearts?"

Hally managed to rein in a groan as she wrote.

"And, yes, of course, two sprigs of parsley," Lou Jay went on excitedly. "Did you know, my students, that parsley freshens the breath? Better than mints, it is—and healthier!" He flourished a finger in the air and popped a morsel into his mouth and chewed. "Also, it brings out that lovely glow, that inner beauty beneath the skin." He slapped his ruddy cheeks, grinning.

"You don't need any help in that area," Ben whispered in her ear.

Irritatingly enough, Hally could feel herself blush with his comment, and she cast him an exasperated sidelong look.

Lou Jay waggled his fingers in time to Beethoven's rumbling tympany. "Now, we get to work. We wash and then we make bouquets garnis."

They all stared at the large mounds of herbs. How many bouquets garnis were they supposed to make, exactly?

And as if reading their thoughts, Lou Jay threw up his hand. "Let all of this be your practicing ground." And with that he produced from the shelf below a giant roll of plastic Baggies. He secured the cheesecloth around the sample bouquet garnis and slid it into the Baggie. He zipped it closed. "And voilà! We are done! Fun, fun, fun!"

"Like my mother says, 'you're not a cook until you know what a bouquet garni is,' " parroted Ben.

"Okay, so I know what it is," said Hally, "but what is it *for?*"

"What I want to know," said Ben out of the side of his mouth, "is what does he do with all this food after we're done with it?"

As they set about making bouquets garnis, a small feeling of panic was slowly uncurling itself in Hally's belly. She needed to learn how to cook, not how to bag herbs. And adding to her vexation was the fact that no one else in the class seemed to care whether they actually got down to cooking a real gourmet meal. It seemed to Hally that everyone—with the exception of Karl MacAvoy and his partner—had begun to pair off, accepting their allotted coupling with a kind of romantic complacency. It sizzled all around her: romance ... love. It was making her crazy.

"Tonight, let Beethoven open the petals of your heart. Ah ... I feel the burgeoning of romance in this kitchen." He opened his eyes and nodded. "Oh, yes, I can see it, smell it, *feel* it—the scent of love."

Hally stared at the chef, with his puffy white chef's hat set crooked upon his rounded head, the thick—albeit graceful—body poised in a ballerina's stance. She blinked, suppressing a snort, and glanced over at Ben. However, her cynical expression swiftly faded when she caught the strange look in her cooking partner's eye.

Chapter Four

Hally shook hands with the owners of Milwaukee Scents. The wife-and-husband team had spent the past half hour arguing about the new potpourri line they were introducing. However, they were impressed by Hally's ability to discern cinnamon from nutmeg, and they liked the idea about incorporating cooking herbs into their inventory.

"You must do a lot of cooking, Miss Chrisswell," said the husband, holding open his wife's coat. "Will you be handling our account from now on?" he asked, helping his wife slip her arms into her coat.

"No, Wade will be returning as soon as his wife has her baby."

The wife buttoned up her coat, flashing Hally a motherly smile. "Family should always come first. You've got a, er—what do you call them these days . . . 'significant other'?"

"Oh, I'm sure she's got a sweetheart stashed away somewhere." The husband winked.

Hally shrugged and shook her head, smiling. "My work takes up most of my time these days," she told them.

The wife glanced at Hally with a mixture of disapproval and sadness, donning the look of a person whose experiences had taught them enough to know when someone was making a mistake. "A career is a fine thing," she said. "But it does not complete you." She linked her arm affectionately in her husband's. "Oh, the two of us—we may fight like cats and dogs, but I don't know what I'd do without my Horst, here."

Horst smiled at his wife, patting her arm. "Our business is important, yes—but we don't let it interfere with family. Did I tell you how Bea and I met . . . ?"

Hally listened politely, and watched their faces suddenly come alive as they relived the long-ago, but still deeply entrenched, memory of their budding romance. They argued over details, but the way they looked at each other, Hally sensed those old sentiments were as strong as when these two people had first met.

After they left, Hally returned to the first floor feeling strangely buoyed and invigorated, a gladness wrapping itself around her heart. She entered the office, whistling, full of energy.

"Wade just called," said Marla. Her eyes sparkled and she grinned broadly. "Karen had the baby! Eight pounds, three ounces, twenty-one inches."

"Are we talking about a baby, or a turkey?" muttered Danny form his desk.

Hally threw an eraser at him. "That's great! Boy or girl?"

"Her name is Ginger Georgina Buchner," announced Marla.

Danny harrumphed. " 'Ginger.' Sounds like the name of a cat."

"It's a good cooking spice," said Hally, laughing.

"Well, I think it's a beautiful name," said Marla. "I thought we would have a baby shower—after I get back from my honeymoon, of course. But our apartment's so small, and with all of Gord's stuff . . ." Marla looked imploringly at Hally.

Hally let out a surrendering sigh. "I suppose we could have it at my place," she said. Hally thought then about the state of her one-bedroom apartment. Granted, it was spacious, clean, and organized, but what had Tina called it? Sterile?

"Oh, before I forget. Tina Kerfoot called while you were at your meeting."

Danny blew his nose. "Hally, you want to look at these mockups for the Nobler Kitty Litter account?"

"You mean, we might actually make the deadline?" Hally grinned.

Danny winced. "Well, Jacob, my eldest, has a hockey tournament beginning this weekend, and Susie's got her sorority benefit Friday afternoons—"

"Danny, I need you with me at that meeting on Friday."

"You and Marla can handle it by yourselves, can't you?"

"I'm getting married on Saturday! I don't need any more pressure." Marla bit her nails, then wrenched them from her mouth. "I'm already a bundle of nerves, as it is!"

"That's why I'm single," muttered Hally, pressing the heel of her hand against her forehead. "Okay, okay. We'll work it out. Let's see those mockups, Danny."

"Your friend, Tina, said it was urgent you call her back," reminded Marla.

Urgent. Everything was "urgent" with Tina. Hally exhaled loudly and reached for the phone.

"Hi, Tina. What's up?"

"Hally! Perfect timing! I was just on my way over to your office," said Tina. "I just wanted to let you know they have a sale on art prints over at Hallowed Ways—and Parker Hardware has twenty-percent discounts off interior paints and wallpaper."

Hally stared blankly at the receiver.

"Anyway," Tina went on, "I thought I'd pick some stuff up for your apartment."

"Huh?"

"Well, you said I could redecorate your place, so I thought—"

"Tina, I said I'd *think* about it—"

"If I start now, it'd be ready in time for that presentation of yours. You're going to need pots and pans—and dishes, too. As I recall, the last time we came over, you were serving wine in coffee mugs—"

"Whoa! Just a second, Tina. Let me think." Hally tugged on her earlobe, gnawing on her lip.

"I could let myself in today. I have some great ideas for your place. What do you think about a European-American, Italian kind of atmosphere?"

"Tina, maybe it's not such a good idea—"

"Hally, I've been working on this since Monday."

"Oh, all right," Hally relented with a grimace. "But nothing too radical or flamboyant—"

"Terrific! I'll see you later!" And Tina hung up.

Hally eyed the receiver in her hand. Uh-oh. Now what had she done? She suddenly had visions of coming home to an apartment crammed full with European trinkets, red-checked tablecloths, velvet mountings of dancing clowns hanging on multicolored walls bordered with stenciled ducks and cows and sunflowers—Oh no, how much was this going to cost her? She'd already doled out a bundle for this gourmet course. Hally hurriedly redialed Tina's number.

There was no answer.

"Trouble?" Danny looked up, noting her worried expression.

"Trouble," muttered Hally, wincing and tugging hard on her earlobe.

Everyone was gathered around Lou Jay in the kitchen when Hally entered the room. Tchaikovsky's *Swan Lake* tiptoed poignantly in the background. As she approached, the other Gourmet Hearts turned to look at her.

The Gourmet Cupid 65

"Ah, and here comes our twelfth Gourmet Heart!" greeted Lou Jay. "Now we are complete."

"You're late," murmured Ben.

Hally narrowed her eyes at him. "Some of us do work," she answered curtly.

"Oh, I thought maybe your boyfriend from the other day held you up."

"I don't have a boyfriend." From the other day? What did he mean by that?

"You go to the Arbre often, do you?"

"What are you talking about?" The Arbre—why did that name sound familiar? And then it suddenly occurred to her. Saturday night. Yes, the Arbre was where Roger Chetner had taken her and Tina and Garry that evening. Hally stole a quick glance at Ben. So he had seen her.

"Please, my Gourmet Hearts. You will all have your turn to create chicken and beef stock. But I would be most grateful for a little less chatter, yes?"

Hally whipped open her notebook and ignored Ben, though she could feel his deep green gaze still intent on her. Her hand went self-consciously to her French braid, and she adjusted her apron around the waist of her navy skirt. At least now they were getting into the nitty-gritty of gourmet cooking.

"Like the heart of romance, there are many mysteries in gourmet cooking," spouted Lou Jay. "But first this evening we will fathom the true essence of chicken stock . . ."

"I think ours tasted the best, don't you think?" Ben rasped, his lips just below Hally's ear. His breath tickled her neck, and she stifled a quiver, resisting an urge to tug on her earlobe.

"I could lick an envelope and it would taste like chicken stock." Hally ran her tongue around her mouth.

"Or beef stock. I can't tell the difference anymore. Why did we have to taste *everyone's*?"

" 'A chef must confront his creation—and his competition.' " quoted Ben, imitating Lou Jay's passionate, slightly accented voice. "What nationality do you think he is, anyway?"

"Swedish-German-Austrian-Russian-Chinese-Italian," said Hally, shrugging tiredly. "I have a feeling Lou Jay's not his real name," she added, gazing down at her notes.

"Sometimes there's a good reason for a person to use ... pseudonyms," said Ben. "You know, for protection."

"Protection from what?" Hally shook her head. "Or it could mean he's hiding something."

Ben glanced at her, a sudden apprehensive look crossing his face. He opened his mouth, as if to comment on this, but he abruptly bit down on his lip and said nothing. He ran his fingers through his hair, looking vaguely uncomfortable.

Lou Jay reappeared from the freezing unit hefting an enormous barrel.

"What's he going to do with thiry frozen containers of beef and chicken stock, anyway?" wondered Ben aloud.

Hally was wondering who was going to wash up all the dishes. She consulted her watch; it was already after eight.

"Now, my Gourmet Hearts, we must cleanse the palate. Miss Chrisswell, I would be most honored if you would help me up here." He beckoned to her, then waved his hands like a symphony conductor as Tchaikovsky regaled in a rain of bellowing trumpets in the background.

Hally reluctantly rose from the couch and positioned

The Gourmet Cupid 67

herself next to Lou Jay. He extracted flute-shaped dessert dishes from the cupboard and handed them to her.

"Tonight, we have lime sherbert—to freshen the mouth, and neutralize the taste buds. One never knows when one is to be kissed, eh?" He winked at Hally and began scooping the lime-green dessert into the dishes. "And Miss Chrisswell, here, will be your server this evening. You may tip her as you see fit." He let out a deep, sonorous laugh.

Hally gazed out at the other Gourmet Hearts, squaring her shoulders and feeling herself grow rigid as her eyes took in Ben's amused grin. The tray was heavy and she carried it carefully, concentrating on her steps.

"Thank you, Hally," said Michael, running his fingers over his slicked-back hair. And he winked at her as he selected a dish off the tray. Immediately, his partner leaned closer to him, her red-painted nails curling possessively over his arm.

Charles and his mousy partner both reached up at the same time, their fingers touching. They giggled and flushed at each other. As they removed the two dishes of sherbet, the tray, unbalanced, seesawed, and the two remaining desserts suddenly slid across and tipped.

"Oops!" Ben caught the dishes, but not before the second one upended its lime-green contents in his lap.

"Oh!" exclaimed Hally.

"Well." Ben gazed down at his lap. "I'm always up for new experiences. Who says I need to eat out of a dish, anyway?"

Hally flung open her briefcase, searching for a Kleenex. She fished out a crumpled handkerchief. "Oh," she muttered with embarrassment when she noted the initials *B.A.* embroidered into the corner. Its center was marked with a large strawberry stain. She handed it to him with a chagrined smile.

"I guess we're even, then," said Ben, wiping up the

sherbet from his pants. "But you know, of course, I can't give you a tip—as pretty a waitress as you are."

"Sorry." But her apology lacked sincerity, and despite the flush that flamed her cheeks, she added, with as much distance and coolness she could muster: "You can share mine, if you like."

Ben's eyebrows lifted. "I'll share whatever your Gourmet Heart desires," he said, his green eyes twinkling.

While they ate, Lou Jay reeled into a lecture about gourmet cookingware. Hally retrieved her pad and began to jot down notes.

" 'Mandoline' is spelled with an 'o,' not an 'e,' " Ben pointed out.

Hally pinched her earlobe and corrected the word.

" 'Ramekin' has only one 'n,' " he told her.

She fixed him with an annoyed glare.

"And 'Julienne' is 'ienne—' "

Hally's poisonous glower shut him up.

"Just trying to help."

"Well, you're not helping. These are *my* notes." She furrowed her brow, trying to hear Lou Jay over the persistent tympanous music and the murmurs of the other Gourmet Hearts.

"I just figured you'd want to do well on the test," said Ben.

"Test?"

Ben grinned. "Hmm . . . seeing you taking down all these notes—well, I was starting to get the feeling you didn't enroll in this class for mere pleasure."

"You're right about that," grumbled Hally. She scratched out the words "cost iran" and rewrote "cast iron." "Please, you're making me lose my concentration."

"Gourmet cooking comes from the heart, not the head," he reminded her.

"Look, you do it your way, and I'll do it my way, okay?"

Lou Jay splayed open his thick arms. "And, of course, the mark of a true professional gourmet chef can be expressed in two words." He paused dramatically. Hally bit her lip and leaned forward in anticipation.

"Orderliness—and cleanliness," he pronounced, turning to the dishes piled up beside the sinks.

"Well, looks like we're on KP duty," said Ben cheerfully.

"I knew this was too good to be true." Hally sighed, reaching over and spooning out the last of the lime sherbert.

A half hour later, Hally pulled the plug on the sink and dried her hands on the apron. Lou Jay had conspicuously absented himself, hiding away somewhere in the back room.

But suddenly he emerged, accompanied by two men dressed in white chef's garments. They moved directly into the walk-in freezing unit, and after a minute came out, carrying familiar-looking containers.

"Hmm . . . now we know what he does with all our hard work," muttered Ben.

Lou Jay grinned at them. "Friday, we learn about the dangerous side of gourmet cooking," he announced. "We will carve and slice and dice and chop." He mimed karatelike movements in the air. "Ah! There are none among you, I hope, who are harboring any pent-up hostility?" He threw back his great round head and laughed.

I wouldn't bet on it, Hally growled to herself. She shrugged on her coat, feeling more tired than she'd felt in a long time. But she hadn't been sleeping well these past few nights, her thoughts keeping her awake, her worries and anxieties invading her dreams. And there was a peculiar ever-present fluttering in her chest and stomach these days, a feeling as though something was about to happen—

"Uh, Hally?" Ben picked up her briefcase and handed it to her. "I was wondering if you wouldn't mind giving me a lift. My, er, car broke down this morning."

Hally gazed at him. *Can't you call Veronica Wilmott?* she asked him silently.

"But, hey, if you have somewhere to go—"

"No, no. No problem," said Hally quickly. Her heart was beating hard all of a sudden, and that irritating fluttering began in her chest again. She forced a composed, calm expression into her face. "No problem," she found herself echoing.

They walked together through the parking lot, and ran into Michael and his slender, high-heeled partner.

"We're going for coffee," said Michael. His attention was focused on Hally as he spoke. "Would you two like to join us? There's this place called the Arbre we wanted to check out—"

"Hally and I've already got plans," said Ben.

Hally glanced over at him, taken aback. "Well, I—"

"Come on, Michael. They have plans." Michael's cooking partner pulled on his arm.

Michael looked disappointed, but he flashed Hally a warm smile. "Some other time, then?"

Hally nodded uncertainly.

Ben climbed into the passenger seat of her Mustang. "Nice car. Neat. Organized. Clean. Yup, just what I expected."

"What do you mean by that?" And in the same breath she blurted, "And what was that all about back there? We don't have any plans together."

"I was doing you a favor. That guy isn't right for you."

"Who are you to tell me who's right for me?" retorted

The Gourmet Cupid 71

Hally indignantly. "I happen to think Michael's a great guy."

"Michael, eh? Oh, I see. So you two've been out together already," said Ben, his tone gruff.

"Not that it's any of your business, but no. I'm—I don't have time to date."

"Well, you know what they say: 'All work and no play makes Hally a—' "

"Where do you want me to drop you off?" interrupted Hally, realizing that she was driving toward her own apartment.

"Your place would be nice." He grinned, then shook his head. "No, the Kingsdale Hotel. I, er, have to meet someone there."

Veronica Wilmott? The name left a bad taste in her mouth. Hally took a hard right down Teutonia Avenue, and Ben reached out to clasp the dashboard, steadying himself.

"So, you're going to go home and work, is that it?" he said, after a moment.

"Yes," she replied tartly.

"But you do take Saturday evenings off, right?"

"Sometimes." She frowned, feeling his eyes watching her. Her stomach jumped a little.

"Saturday night it is, then."

"I don't think I'm free—"

"I'll pick you up at seven."

Hally stared at the dashboard. "You don't even know where I live."

"I'll find it. But it'd be a lot easier if you gave me the address."

"Uh—"

"There. It's settled. Seven o'clock, Saturday night." Ben picked up a piece of unopened junk mail shoved between the gearshift and the seat. He read out her address. "Great. Believe it or not, I have a photographic memory—especially for important things." He turned the envelope over in his hands. "Hey! You'd better open this. It says here you could be the next million-dollar sweepstakes winner!"

Hally snatched it out of his hands.

"So, I bet someone like you knows how to ice skate really well," he said.

"Ice skate?"

"Don't tell me you don't know how to skate."

"Of course I do," Hally answered gruffly, without thinking. But the last time she'd been on skates was, well ... she couldn't remember, exactly. She nosed the Mustang into the Kingsdale Hotel lot, and sidled up to the entrance.

Ben opened the passenger door, and the car light danced for a moment in his eyes. "Thanks, Hally. I appreciate this." He smiled. "I'll see you Saturday night—oh, but we have our 'dangerous' gourmet class on Friday, don't we?"

And before Hally could reply, he slammed the door and hurried up the Kingsdale Hotel steps.

"Dangerous" gourmet class, indeed, she thought, tugging on her earlobe.

She couldn't get the apartment door open. "What the—"

"Oh, just a minute, Hal!" Tina's face peered at her through the crack.

Hally heard her grunt and shuffle something away from the doorway. "Okay! Come on in!"

Hally stepped inside and blinked.

"All right, before you say anything, I just want to let you know I got all this stuff on sale," said Tina, wiping her hands on her coveralls. "I know it looks like a mess right now, but it'll look great when it's finished. I promise."

The Gourmet Cupid 73

Hally nodded mutely as she stepped over the paint cans and paint trays. She gazed, speechless, at the paint-speckled canvas draped along the floor.

"I lost track of time," Tina went on quickly. "I wasn't sure when you'd be back from your class. I feel so invigorated! Oh—watch your step, there." Hally side-stepped one of the trays, and paused to stare at the far living room wall.

"Pale terra-cotta," said Tina, following her friend's gaze. "You like it? It's a sort of glazing, 'pushing' technique I came up with. Gives the room a kind of artsy, European feel, don't you think?"

"Uh, yes. It's, er—"

"This apartment has great ceilings. And I never really noticed these beautiful Victorian moldings. You know what this place reminds me of? Mary Tyler Moore's apartment." Tina replaced the lids on the paint cans. "Oh, and Roger Chetner called. I would've let the answering machine take it, but I thought it might be Garry again."

"What—what'd he want?" Hally searched about for a place to set down her briefcase.

"Well, I didn't think I was going to be here this late. I forgot the twins had swimming lessons tonight," said Tina, grimacing. But her eyes shone with excitement. "I also forgot how much I love doing this."

"No, I mean Roger Chetner. What'd he want?"

Tina laughed. "Sorry, I'm just so excited about all this. Roger wanted to know if you were free Saturday night. He just winged some tickets to *Mame*." She glanced at Hally. "He invited Garry and I as well, so—"

"I can't make it Saturday night." *I have a date with Ben Atkinson.*

"Gee, you look beat, Hal! Wait—what do you mean you can't make it for Saturday night—oh, right! You have that wedding to go to." Tina bit her lip. "Rats! I forgot. Well, I wrote down Roger's number. It's by the phone.''

Marla's wedding! Hally tugged on her earlobe. It had completely slipped her mind!

"I made some coffee," Tina went on. "You know, if you're going to cook for these people, you're definitely going to need to invest in some pots and pans, a good set of knives—Hey! We could go shopping this Friday, if you like.''

"I have class."

"Right, right. I forgot. Mondays, Wednesdays, and Fridays," said Tina, looking thoughtful. "How'd it go tonight, anyway?"

Hally hung up her coat wearily. "We made chicken and beef stock." *And washed dishes,* she added with a silent groan: *And Ben Atkinson asked me out on a date.*

"Great. Pretty soon you'll be whipping up things like duck à l'orange and veal scallopini—and then, *you* can have Garry and me over for dinner. Or Roger." She eyed her friend coyly. "Or maybe . . . your cooking partner. What's his name again?"

"Ben Atkinson." Hally forced a blank expression into her face. But she could feel her ears go scarlet.

"Has he asked you out yet?"

"What makes you think he'd ask me out?"

"Your face just went beet red a second ago when you said his name." Tina grinned as Hally's hands went to her cheeks. "Aha! So he *did* ask you out."

"Tina—" But Hally grinned despite her embarrassment. She could never hide anything from this woman, who appeared to have X-ray vision when it came to Hally's innermost feelings. "I thought you were all gung ho about me getting together with Roger Chetner."

Tina shrugged. "Hey, I know what it's like when two people of the opposite sex are thrust together. After all, that's how Garry and I fell in love, remember?" Her dark brown eyes glazed over for a moment, a nostalgic smile passing across her heart-shaped face. "What made me take that rock-climbing class, I don't know. Maybe it was fate. Maybe it was fate that I slipped and pulled my hamstring that day."

Hally nodded, having heard this story a zillion times already. "Garry carried you all the way to the hospital—"

"And he waited there for over two hours." Tina sighed. "I knew from that moment I hobbled out of that hospital that he was the one." She slowly combed her fingers through her curly hair. "And two months later, we were married."

Hally rolled her eyes. "Tina, I think you're getting a little ahead of yourself. Ben and I are just... cooking partners."

Tina flashed her friend a knowing smile. "So when are you and this Ben Atkinson going out?"

Hally was too tired to keep skirting around Tina's inquiries. She told him about going skating with him Saturday night.

"Skating? Now that's romantic. Aw, but you have that wedding on Saturday." Tina waggled her brows. "Well, you could always ask him to the wedding," she added with a slow, sly grin. "Wow, Hally. Your love life has definitely taken on an interesting twist. Two men in one day!"

Three, Hally amended silently. *Let's not forget Michael*—but she doubted his cooking partner would let him anywhere near Hally. Not that Hally was really interested in the man with the slicked-back hair anyway. But the attention she was getting from him was somehow... satisfying, she thought, remembering Ben Atkinson's reaction. Surely, Ben wasn't... jealous?

Hally silently guffawed at this thought.

Tina sighed wistfully. "It takes me back to my single days..."

Hally rolled fitfully back and forth under her covers. Her thoughts were like derby cars racing down the tracks of her mind, intermittently smashing and colliding into one another, vying for the lead position. And finally, in a fit of annoyance, she flicked on the bedside light and tramped out into the kitchen to make herself some cocoa.

She shivered in her thin cotton pajamas. The November chill had seeped into her apartment, and outside a windstorm of leaves buffeted her windows. She'd have to call the landlord to see about turning up the heat.

Beneath her feet the paint canvas crackled and rumpled about her ankles, impeding her step. She stubbed her toe on a paint can and stifled a yell. Drawing in a breath, she limped into the kitchen and felt for the light switch.

The brightness of the stark white primer on the walls hurt her eyes. Squinting, she pulled down a mug from the cupboard, and as she moved to the refrigerator, her eye fell to a narrow brown package poking out between the space in the counter cabinet. She bent down and slid it out.

Scrawled on the brown paper wrapping was the word "kitchen." Hally inspected it and surmised it to be a print of some kind. She groaned. Tina was certainly taking liberties. *Please,* she thought, *let it not be something too outrageous.* Carefully, and with a little trepidation, she picked off the tape and unwrapped the brown covering.

A very large tomato stared at her. Hally blinked. Why, it was beautiful! A crackle glaze had been applied to the surface to give it a Renaissance-like feel, the simplicity of its subject—Hally brought her face closer, her gaze suddenly drawn to the upper right corner.

The Gourmet Cupid

A tiny winged cupid grinned, his bow empty. Hally followed the direction of the cherub's hand and immediately found its target: a man and a woman, dressed in contemporary clothing, lay partially hidden in the leafy stem of the enormous tomato. They were locked in an amorous embrace.

Hally sighed. She should have known Tina wouldn't be able to resist something like this; Tina's heart was incurably diseased with romance.

Hally laid the painting on the counter, shaking her head. Her gaze strayed from the couple to glare at the cupid, who smiled back at her triumphantly.

"Keep your arrows to yourself, little cupid," muttered Hally.

She made her cocoa and paused to glance about the living room. Her sofa and matching love seat whimpered beneath the plastic covering, their plainness already appearing to succumb to the transformation of the far wall. Hally felt her stomach lurch. What was happening to her conservative, orderly life?

As she climbed back into the warmth of her bed, she retrieved from her briefcase the Bel Abner file, thick now with photocopies of news clippings and magazine articles. She glanced at the clock on her bedside table: 1:21 A.M. Tomorrow she had an eight o'clock conference, her first executive meeting. Hally yawned and rubbed her eyes. It wouldn't do to make her debut as acting AE looking like a myopic zombie. She'd just read for a while, she thought. . . .

Chapter Five

Hally jolted awake. The light from her night table spilled across her bed, and after her head cleared, she realized she was still sitting upright. The contents of the Bel Abner file she'd been reading lay splayed across her legs. Her eyes darted to the clock.

"Oh, no! I'm going to be late!" She leaped out of bed and a stab of pain rocketed up her spine. The back of her neck throbbed, making her flinch as she reached down to collect the strewn clippings from the bed and the floor.

Hunched over, she dashed into the bathroom, and quickly washed her face. She cursed aloud. There was no time for a shower. She knotted her hair into a bun at the back of her head and grabbed her makeup bag.

It was this darn Bel Abner campaign, she thought, racing for the door. *And that stupid gourmet class*. If only she hadn't met Ben Atkinson—

No, it was just her timing; her timing was off, that was all, she reassured herself.

"Hally! I need you to look over these comps—Hel-looo! Earth to Hally. Come in, please." Danny snapped his fingers under her nose.

"Huh? Oh, sorry. I'm not quite awake yet, I guess." Hally yawned, then winced as the soreness in her neck intensified with the action. She kneaded the muscles, groaning.

The Gourmet Cupid

"Executive conference was that boring, huh?" said Danny. "Or do you have a hangover?"

Hally gave him a sour look. "I didn't get much sleep last night."

"Oh? Anyone I know?"

Marla looked up from her desk, her expression alert. "Does this mean you're bringing a date to the wedding?" She chewed on her nails, then forced them from her lips with a harrassed grimace. "The Bonners just told me they can't come, so I rearranged the table settings, but I can call—"

"No, don't worry, Marla. I won't bring a date," Hally assured her wearily.

"Really, it's no problem, Hally." Marla picked up the phone. "We have to pay for the settings, anyway— whether the guests come or not."

"So who's the guy?" Danny propped his elbows on her desk. "He's gotta be pretty special. I've never seen you look this bad since you came down with the Hong Kong flu."

"I look that bad?"

Danny grinned. "Naw, you just look like the rest of us deadbeats. It's nice to see you looking not so, you know . . . perfect—in control, like you always seem to be." He harrumphed. "But the opposite sex will do that to you: drive you a little crazy. I was wondering when you'd finally come over to the dark side." He laughed.

The dark side, thought Hally ominously. Could it be Danny was right? Ben Atkinson suddenly pushed his way into her thoughts, his deep green eyes twinkling, the wry, full mouth turned up into a playful grin. It was the way his coat hung across his broad shoulders, the heady smell of him, making her nostrils flare—

"Okay! It's done!" said Marla, slamming down the receiver.

Hally frowned. "What's done?"

Danny rubbed his hands together. "So we'll finally be able to meet Hally's 'Mystery Man.' This should be good."

"Mystery Man? No, wait. You don't understand—"

"Okay, enough about your love life," said Danny impatiently. "We have a presentation deadline tomorrow, remember? The Nobler Kitty Litter account? And I hear these women can be a tad finicky." He grinned and pointed to the art boards on her desk. "So, what do you think?"

I think my life has just become a little too complicated. Hally massaged her temples with a groan.

"Hello?"

"Hally, it's Roger Chetner. I just wanted to confirm for Saturday night."

Hally slumped down on her sofa. The sound of the plastic covering startled her for an instant. She gazed about at the paint cans, brushes, and rollers strewn about her apartment. She heard Tina humming in the kitchen, doing who-knew-what with the wallpaper.

"Hally?"

"Uh, hi, Roger. I was going to call you," she said, suppressing a yawn. "Unfortunately, I can't make it Saturday night. I have a wedding to go to."

"Oh, that's too bad."

Hally heard the disappointment in his voice.

"Well, I know how swamped you are with work," he said after a moment. "I'm really busy myself. It's all I can do to find one night a week free. Maybe we can go out next Saturday night—oh, no, I have a business meeting that night . . . How about the Saturday after that—no, wait. What am I thinking? That's Thanksgiving weekend, isn't it? I'm taking an out-of-town client to Menomonee Falls."

Hally heard the sound of pages ruffling in the back-

The Gourmet Cupid 81

ground as Roger flipped through his appointment book. "But I'm free the Saturday after that. Would you like to do something—go to dinner, perhaps? Or maybe we could take in a show? Whatever you want."

Hally rubbed her tired eyes. Her head was reeling, trying to catch up—or rather, untangle herself from Roger's whirlwind of a schedule. "Why don't you, uh, call me that week, then. And then we . . . we'll see what happens."

"Great. I'm all for spontaneity. So I'll just pencil you in for that day," said Roger. "You know, Hally, not every woman would be so understanding. But you and I are similar that way, aren't we? Our work is important to us, and sometimes we just have to make sacrifices."

"Yes," Hally replied woodenly.

As she rang off, Tina emerged from the kitchen. "So that was Roger? When are you two getting together?"

Hally gazed at her friend distractedly. She shrugged. Roger's phone call had already fled from her thoughts. "Next month, maybe."

"Next month?"

"He penciled me in."

Tina sighed, stroking her chin with a pasty finger. "Hmm . . . I can't see this working between you two, Hally. He's obviously too involved with his work."

"I thought you said he was perfect for me."

"I don't know. Maybe you need someone to take you away from all this."

"I love my work, Tina. It's what I do—what I am. Granted, it does tend to consume a lot of my time—"

"Speaking of which, I'd better get moving. Garry and I promised to take the kids to a movie tonight." Tina wiped her hands on her coveralls. She glanced about the apartment. "Sorry about the inconvenience. But wait until it's finished. You won't recognize the place."

That's what I'm afraid of, thought Hally, yawning.

She was desperate for a hot soak in the tub, but the Nobler Kitty Litter presentation was scheduled for tomorrow afternoon, and it appeared as though she would be doing it solo, without Wade.

And then there was the Bel Abner file to go through; Danny and Marla had come up with some interesting campaign ideas worth looking into. And she also wanted to practice making chicken and beef stock while it was still fresh in her mind.

That darn résumé of hers; all her problems thus far had precipitated from that one tiny white lie. Who knew that one teeny fib could turn her life upside-down—cause her so much grief? What on earth had possessed her to tell them she was a gourmet cook in the first place?

"So, we still on for Sunday?" Tina's question jarred Hally out of her thoughts. Tina rolled up her coveralls. "There's this place downtown: Culinary Cookware, I think it's called. They're supposed to specialize in gourmet stuff."

Hally nodded. "I think I already know what I need." She reached inside her briefcase. "I've got it all written down—where is that notepad?" She searched through her files, but her notebook wasn't there. "Oh, blast it!"

"Have you got the menu prepared yet? You know, the other night we tried that Bel Abner Gourmet Blue Cheese Sauce. It's really quite delicious," said Tina, buttoning up her coat. "They make spices, too, don't they?"

"Maybe I should get *you* to make the dinner," grumbled Hally, still trying to find her notepad. Where had she put it? Had it fallen out in the car? Had she left it at the lodge? This was the second item she'd lost in the past couple of weeks. And the research department's copy of *Life Worth Living* still hadn't shown up. She berated herself again for not getting the broken clasp on her briefcase fixed.

The Gourmet Cupid 83

Tina waved good-bye. "Have fun at the wedding. Say, did you ask your cooking partner—uh—"

"Ben Atkinson."

"Right. Did you ask him to the wedding yet."

Not yet, answered Hally silently. "Tina, I don't know . . . I have to think about it." Was she nuts? She couldn't ask a total stranger to a wedding. And anyway, would he go? A wedding was so . . . personal, and they barely knew each other. She didn't even know what he did for a living—if indeed, he did anything.

Danny had unknowingly been right on the nose when he'd referred to Ben as her "Mystery Man," Hally mused. Was that what made her cooking partner so appealing to her? she wondered. Was it the mystery of him that piqued her interest?

After Tina left, Hally traipsed cautiously across the canvas tarp and strode into the kitchen. In the refrigerator two bottles of relish, an old crusty jar of mustard, and a carton of milk gazed back at her forlornly. She opened the crisper and extracted a suspect-looking apple which trembled and gushed in her palm. She threw it out, and opened the freezer, pulling out the last remaining frozen dinner with a sigh.

After work tomorrow, she'd go grocery shopping. She'd force herself through the fresh-produce section, maybe pick up some spices—

But then she remembered: cooking class. So she'd skip this one, she thought. But she knew she'd have to attend; she'd gotten this far, after all. And she might miss something vitally important.

However, as she plodded into her den and began arranging the Nobler Kitty Litter mockups on her desk, Hally realized that, in truth, she *wanted* to go to her gourmet cooking class—that she was actually looking forward to it.

But why? Surely not because of Ben Atkinson?

Hally forced her attention back to the mockups, not answering this. No, it was better not to get involved, and to let her Mystery Man remain a mystery, she thought decidedly.

The representatives of Nobler Kitty Litter, three women garbed in earth-tone hemp garments, sporting cat-shaped earrings and necklaces, brooches, and jangling bracelets with tiny cat charms, listened to Hally uncertainly. They were used to dealing with Wade, and Hally could feel the tension grow in the room as she went on.

"Do you have a cat, Miss Chrisswell?" one of them interrupted.

"Uh, no, I don't."

They exchanged glances, a silent conversation passing between them.

"Perhaps we'd better wait for Mr. Buchner," said the woman, rising. "It's not that we don't like your ideas, Miss Chrisswell. But I think we'd all much prefer to deal with Wade." The others nodded in agreement.

Hally tugged on her earlobe, hoping her professional smile successfully hid her disappointment.

"I hope you don't take this as a personal insult, Miss Chrisswell," said the woman with the cat-charm bracelet, shaking her hand. "You understand, we have a rapport with Wade—and well, he understands what we want."

"No—no problem," said Hally. "It's just that Wade won't be back—"

"Wade's not leaving Necessitas, is he?"

Just this morning, the news circulating about the office had Wade stepping down from his executive position. Supposedly, he was leaving the team and moving into another department; his advertising executive job was now up for grabs.

"No, he's not exactly leaving Necessitas—"

The Gourmet Cupid 85

"Good. Because I have to admit, Wade was the reason we signed on at Necessitas in the first place." Hally shook the hands of the other two women. "Anyway, thank you for your time, Miss Chrisswell."

Hally trudged to her office, her stomach churning. She'd seen the determined look in those women's faces. If Wade did decide to permanently leave the team, to step down from the executive chair, they would lose Nobler Kitty Litter. And it was presently one of their team's biggest accounts.

She gazed about the empty office, her head throbbing. She picked up a jar of Bel Abner Gourmet Béarnaise Sauce, turning it over in her hands. Bel Abner was her big chance—her *only* chance, now. She'd blown the Nobler Kitty Litter account, but Bel Abner could save her.

She dialed Wade's number and left a brief message on his answering machine to call her back.

An hour later the phone rang.

"Hey, there! How's my AE replacement doing?"

"Wade, nobody can replace you. Listen, about the Nobler Kitty Litter account—"

"Hold on a sec, will ya, Hal?" A wail pierced through the receiver. "Little tyke's hungry again. Who would've thought such a tiny thing could eat so much? Eat and sleep, that's all she does. But I swear, she is the cutest baby. You should have one, Hally. Makes you suddenly wake up to what's really important in your life."

"Yeah, sure. I'm on it," began Hally awkwardly. The last thing she needed in her life was a *family*. "I spoke with the representatives of Nobler Kitty Litter, and, well . . . they'd like you to get in touch with them."

"You haven't heard? I resigned my position earlier today. I'm downshifting into the research department. It's fewer hours and it'll give me more time to spend with the family."

Hally bit her lip, tugging hard on her earlobe. "These

women from Nobler Kitty Litter won't work with anyone but you, Wade. Couldn't you—"

"Aw, Hally. I'm sure you can woo them. I've seen you in action. You're the hardest, most conscientious worker I know. And that's what I told Serina. Act surprised when they offer you the AE job, okay?"

Oh, I'll be surprised, all right, thought Hally miserably.

"Gotta go. Leila's calling me. Hey, and good luck with the Bel Abner campaign. I know you'll do great!" And he hung up.

Hally stared at the phone, wincing. She flipped through Wade's Rolodex and found the number for the Nobler Kitty Litter Association. Just as she went to pick up the receiver, the phone buzzed.

"Hally? It's Serina. Can you make your way over to my office, this afternoon?" The voice sounded clipped and curt.

Hally swallowed. Her headache crawled slowly from her brow, pounding across her skull to settle at the nape of her neck. Reluctantly, she pushed herself out of her chair, and smoothed out the folds in her skirt. Her instincts were already telling her Nobler Kitty Litter had canceled their account.

They'd lost the Nobler Kitty Litter account, but Serina still seemed confident Hally could handle the Bel Abner campaign.

"It's a hectic time of year for everyone. What is it about the holidays that gets us so tense?" Serina had mused, leading Hally out of the office.

"Thanksgiving's supposed to be a time to give thanks—feel thankful for what we have, and instead we end up strangling each other." Serina let out a long-suffering sigh. "Aaah! But don't get me started on

Christmas!" And before Hally could say anything Serina had squeezed her hand.

"Oh, Hally. What I wouldn't give to be in your shoes: single, free to date whomever you choose, not having to deal with all that family hoopla, no obligations, no responsibilities—" A smile of resignation broke across her expression, the dark eyes softening slightly at the corners.

"Hmm . . . the grass is always greener." Serina gave a small laugh, and in that moment, Hally had seen a new youthfulness emerge in the pale face. "But, you know? If I had to do it all over again? I'd do it all exactly the same. In a heartbeat."

Hally had tried to apologize about the Nobler Kitty Litter account, but Serina just waved a dismissive hand.

"We've got bigger fish to fry, Hally."

Hally nosed in front of a slow-moving Taurus, then cut off the truck in the next lane. It honked at her angrily. She ignored it and glanced at the digital clock on the dashboard. She was ten minutes late for class. This day was not going well.

She was aware that her being single, not having to deal with all that "family hoopla," as Serina had put it—had a lot to do with her being assigned as the advertising executive to the Bel Abner campaign. However, Serina had made it quite clear that she had faith in Hally's ability to handle the position.

"It would be a real coup for Necessitas to land this account. Bel Abner carries with it enough prestige—not to mention a huge cash flow—which heaven knows, we need right now," Serina had told her frankly. "And I have a feeling you're just the person to put us back in the game."

Hally massaged her neck as she parked the car before Humboldt Lodge. She turned on the interior light and made a quick search for her notepad. It wasn't there.

She locked her briefcase in the trunk and hurried inside the lodge.

The Gourmet Hearts were milling around the kitchen where Lou Jay was demonstrating chopping techniques. Ben waved and immediately stepped aside to make room for her.

"Hard day at the office, honey?" he whispered in her ear.

She cast a harsh, harried look in his direction.

Lou Jay balanced the knife on his middle finger, twirled it in the air, and deftly caught the handle, then proceeded to chop the carrot on the counter. The knife, Hally observed, was a menacing-looking blade she would've guessed psychotics might wield to butcher their victims, rather than use to chop vegetables. Everyone stared, entranced by Lou Jay's performance, and applauded in amazement.

"You might want this." Ben slipped her notepad into her hand.

Hally stared at him, bunched up her lips suspiciously, and managed to mutter a barely audible "Thanks."

Her pen marked the page inside, and Hally flipped it open. An unrecognizable scrawl took up half of the page. At the bottom, in large capital letters, was a question: *WHAT COLOR ARE YOUR EYES, ANYWAY?*

Hally flushed, avoiding his gaze. She must have left the notepad behind in the room on Wednesday, she thought. But in the same instant, Hally vividly recalled stuffing it into her briefcase that night—just as she had the research department's copy of *Life Worth Living* that first class. However, the magazine had yet to surface.

"So? What color *are* your eyes?"

Hally blinked at him. "Red," she murmured wearily.

". . . the bolster, you see, is important in that it gives the knife more weight when you slice it forward," Lou Jay told them as Chopin's piano keys chopped along in

The Gourmet Cupid

time to Lou Jay's blade. "This motion actually parts the molecules as you are cutting. See? Easy, no?"

It didn't look easy to Hally; it looked dangerous.

"Tuck in your fingers like so, and use your knuckles to guide the knife. Human flesh and blood do not make for a good seasoning—Yaaah!" he suddenly screamed, and everyone recoiled from the counter in horror.

Lou Jay held up his hand and let out a great roaring bellow. "Ah! Be still my Gourmet Hearts. Just a little joke, eh? See? Five fingers." He wiggled his sausagelike fingers at them.

Hally hissed between her teeth, and saw that Ben, too, was grimacing.

"But you notice how I use the knife like a pivot." Lou Jay brought out a stalk of celery and held the blade of the knife, tip down on the board, and began to chop the celery, bringing the knife down in a swift and smooth rocking motion.

Hally scribbled quick notes beneath Ben's nearly illegible scrawl. She observed the tape recorder next to her, and turned to meet the intent gaze of the journalist, Karl MacAvoy.

"It's a lot easier this way," he murmured, indicating the minirecorder. "You don't end up misquoting anybody." The journalist glanced over at Ben, then lowered his voice to a whisper. "By the way, we pay very well for inside information. And our sources are held in the utmost and strictest confidentiality."

Hally frowned, glancing at him curiously.

Lou Jay demonstrated how to cut cabbage, first slicing it into thin strips, then rolling each leaf firmly like a jelly roll, then slicing them again. He trimmed carrots and cucumbers and zucchini into neat rectangular blocks, then cut them into julienned strips. They watched, sucking in their breaths, as he chopped parsley and chives, tomatoes, mushrooms, and onions—all, it seemed, in a matter of mere seconds.

"Now, it is your turn to practice." Lou Jay reached below him and set down two knife blocks, each holding six shiny dangerous-looking knives. "I trust no one here has any ill feelings toward their partners."

Hally glanced over at Ben, who held up his hands in a gesture of playful surrender, grinning. He bent his head toward her. "I trust you, cooking partner."

I'm not sure I can say the same, Hally retorted silently.

Each Gourmet Heart couple was relegated to different stations in the kitchen. Hally and Ben gazed at the mound of cucumbers and carrots and zucchini. Taped to the wall were pictured instructions on how to slice the vegetables, julienne-style.

"Gee." Hally looked at the huge butcherlike knife in her hand. "Couldn't we start with something smaller, like an axe—or a scythe?"

"I thought all advertising executives wielded dangerous weapons." Ben snorted.

"What's that supposed to mean?"

"I don't know—Hey! watch it! Save your aggression for the vegetables."

"I am not aggressive." *I'm nervous,* she thought, *and it's not the knife that's making me nervous.*

Hally selected a cucumber, and Ben picked up a zucchini. They began to slice them—slowly. In the midst of their chopping, they both glanced up at the instructions taped to the wall, and looked at each other. Ben smiled uncertainly, mirroring her own expression. They tittered.

"This is ridiculous." Hally started to giggle.

Ben grunted as he hacked awkwardly at the zucchini. "At the rate we're going, the guests will have already hit old age and have picked out their cemetery plots," he grumbled. A rebellious piece of zucchini slid off the board and ricocheted off the wall. Hally let loose a loud laugh and immediately covered her mouth.

"I think cucumbers are easier," he growled.

Hally was surprised at her own deftness, and equally pleased by how easily she could manipulate the knife. Although her speed was nowhere near that of Lou Jay's, her resulting juliennned strips were neat and perfectly trimmed.

"I think my blade is dull," said Ben in frustration. His efforts had resulted in a pulpy mess of jagged zucchini strips.

"You just have to concentrate—pay attention."

"You sound like my father."

"Your father sounds like a wise man. I'm guessing you don't take after him."

Ben grabbed a cucumber and watched Hally cut the zucchini into precise blocks, then slice them into perfect strips. "No, my brother's more like my old man. I guess you could say I'm the black sheep of the family."

"And your father wants you and your brother to take over the family business, is that it?"

"Hmm . . . something like that. And, well, lately, I've been thinking that it's not such a crazy idea." He glanced at her, and a strange gleam came into his green eyes. "There seems to be an, uh, interesting sideline to it all. Particularly now that a new player has surfaced into the game."

Hally's brows drew together, not understanding. "You mean, your father's business is not what you thought it was?" *Or does this have something to do with Veronica Wilmott?* Suspicion and frustration nagged at her thoughts. *Why won't he just tell me what business his family is in?* And something tightened in her chest as she suddenly conjured up an image of Ben and Veronica together.

"I mean, I've never been interested in things like

number crunching—you know, balancing budgets, profit margins—all that accounting stuff. That's what my brother, Stew, does." Ben struggled ineffectually to keep the blocks of cucumbers together.

"But I found out that there's another side to running a large business like my father's. Public relations, for one." He glanced up at the directions on the wall. "Well, you know all about that. Being in advertising, that is."

He said it was a "large business," thought Hally. "And I guess you get to drink all the beer you want, right?" she ventured.

Ben shot her a quizzical glance.

Okay, his father obviously doesn't own a brewery company. Maybe movie theaters? "Or rather, I meant you get to watch all those movies for free," she said, more a question than a statement.

But her cooking partner's laugh told her she was still off base.

"All right. I give up," Hally shook her head. "What business is you fam—"

"Oh, my, my," Lou Jay put his big hands on their shoulders and shook his head, tsk-tsking forlornly at Ben's butchered pieces of cucumber. "Chopping food is like kissing. Take your time—don't rush. Enjoy yourself. Caress the food with the knife. Concentrate, Mr. Atkinson."

Hally sliced a carrot and it zipped across the counter.

"And you, Miss Chrisswell." He squeezed her shoulder. "Be patient. Let your heart guide you, and I promise you won't be disappointed."

Hally nodded with a sheepish smile. Why was it this strange man always had to drag her heart into everything? She was here to learn how to cook, not to fall in love with food—or *anyone*, for that matter. She stole a furtive glance at her cooking partner, and found, much to her dismay and fury, that she was blushing.

Ben was silent for a moment after Lou Jay moved on to observe Charles and his mousy partner. Hally attacked another carrot, and julienned it perfectly. But her concentration wavered, and she knicked her knuckle while chopping up a zucchini.

"Hey! You all right? Lemme see."

"It's just a scrape," said Hally, sucking at the cut.

"Well, let's see it. Here." He fished a handkerchief from his jeans pocket. The embroidered letters *B. A.* undulated over her fingers.

Hally shook her head. "It's okay. The knife just touched the skin."

Ben yanked her hand out of her mouth. "Gee, you're stubborn. You won't let anybody help you, will you?" He inspected the small cut. "It's just a scrape. You'll live."

She snatched her hand back. "Thank you, Doctor Zhivago, for that amazing diagnosis."

"Well, you know, now that you mention it, you do look a bit like Julie Christie," said Ben with a teasing grin. "Except for the eyes. Ever since I met you I've been trying to figure out what color they are. One minute they look kind of hazel, and then the next, they're like ... tiger's eyes."

"I have sharp teeth, too." She glared at him fiercely.

"And claws, too, no doubt."

Hally was about to retort when Lou Jay trumpeted loudly, prompting the partners to move on to the next station.

Cabbage heads formed a dissarranged pyramid on the counter. The already chopped cabbage filled less than a quarter of the colander. Hally squinted at the pictures on the wall.

"Somebody's going to get a lot of indigestion tonight," said Ben, gazing at the cabbage heads.

"So here we chop up all this food, and then what happens to it?" Hally sliced off the end of the cabbage head. "You think Lou Jay sells it?"

"To his own restaurant?"

"He owns a restaurant?"

Ben gazed at her, surprised. "He owns the Arbre. You didn't know? I thought you went there a lot."

"I don't go there *a lot*. I've been there exactly once, as a matter of fact."

"Oh, don't tell me your *GQ* boyfriend doesn't take you there. I've seen him at the Arbre often enough. It seems to be his favorite lunching spot."

"Well, obviously he's not the only person who likes that place," she said haughtily. *So, just how often do you take Veronica Wilmott to the Arbre?* she was tempted to ask. "And Roger is not my boyfriend," she added.

"Roger, eh? Good thing you and he aren't an item. I wasn't looking forward to a battle on the skating rink."

"Skating rink?" Hally suddenly remembered. "Oh, yes. Uh, I—I can't make it tomorrow."

"Don't tell me you have to work, because I'm afraid I'm just going to have come over to your apartment and kidnap you—"

"No, I have a wedding."

"You're getting married?"

Hally rolled her eyes. "A friend of mine from work is getting married tomorrow. I'm a bridesmaid."

"A friend from work?"

"Marla's a copywriter. We work together at Necessitas." Hally hesitated. Should she ask him? She drew a breath. "If you like—uh, well, you could come to the reception. That is, if you're not too busy," she added quickly. She chopped at the cabbage, feeling her head pound with the motion of the knife.

The Gourmet Cupid 95

"So, I suppose there'll be a lot of people from Necessitas at this wedding," he said, scratching his head.

"Hey, if you don't like weddings—"

"No, no. I'll come." He smiled at her, then suddenly furrowed his brow. "Your boyfriend Roger's not going to be there, is he?"

Hally paused in her chopping. "I told you he's not my boyfriend. Are you afraid of him, or something?"

"It's not him I'm afraid of," he muttered. "Just so there's no misunderstanding here—you're inviting me to this wedding, right?"

"What—you're not used to women asking you out?"

"Not by women who work themselves to death, and especially not by women who have incredibly beautiful eyes, no."

Just gorgeous television stars like Veronica Wilmott, I bet, Hally retorted to herself.

"So?" she prompted finally when he didn't say anything. Now she was beginning to regret the invitation. He was thinking about it too much; obviously he was trying to muster up a polite response to turn her down.

"Okay, sure. I've got an appointment tomorrow afternoon, but I can make the reception. Where is it?"

"Actually, the same place where I dropped you off. The, uh, Kingsdale Hotel."

"The Kingsdale Hotel," mused Ben. He grimaced and scratched his head again.

Hally cocked her head, observing his thoughtful expression. "Is there a problem?"

"Problem? No..." A half-smile sported across his face. "No problem."

But a surge of doubt flitted into her mind as Hally returned to her cabbage. Something was obviously troubling him. Yet, what it was, she couldn't rightly guess. This man was still a puzzle to her, and she realized, as she snuck a look over at him, that she didn't have nearly all the pieces yet.

Chapter Six

Hally cast an eye about the room. From where she sat at the head table, she had a good view of all the guest tables. Everything had a faint pinkish hue, the rose-colored tablecloths blending in with the pink-rosebud-and-carnation centerpieces. The bows were white and pink, tipped with traces of gold and silver sparkles. Tiny candle bulbs set in pale pink shades reflected up into the ceiling crystal chandeliers. Hally followed the waiters in pink bow ties who drifted about like ghosts, refilling the guests' champagne glasses and silently slipping away dishes.

Her sweeping eye paused at an empty seat at the table where sat Serina Heineault and her husband, Rudy. Rudy was beckoning to their sons who were wrestling over in the corner by the wedding cake. Serina caught Hally's searching gaze and tipped her glass.

Hally smiled and gave a small wave.

"Don't those bows look hideous? I told them not *silver*—oh, but what can you do?" Marla sighed, tossing back her veil. "So how's the food? I should've had you come along to help me select the meal. The squab's a little tough, don't you think?"

It's like leather, thought Hally, eyeing the meat. "No, it's delicious, Marla. Everything's perfect. It's a, uh, beautiful wedding."

"So, Hally, when do we get to meet your Mystery

Man? I didn't meet him in the receiving line already, did I? What's his name?"

They were interrupted by the sound of clinking glasses. Marla returned to the center chair where Gord rose, circled his arms about her shoulder and waist, and dipped her, kissing his new wife passionately. Marla's hand went to her veil, and she laughed as it fell into her maid of honor's lap.

Gord's brother, who was seated next to Hally, leaned over. Nervous sweat beaded his forehead and he smiled awkwardly. "So you work with Marla?"

Hally nodded and smiled politely.

"Some wedding, huh?"

"Yes. Beautiful."

He paused, running his finger along the collar of his shirt. "Known Marla long?"

Hally was about to respond, but she was in that instant saved by a waiter who approached her and tapped her gently on the shoulder: "Miss Hally Chrisswell?"

"Yes?"

"A gentleman asked me to give this to you." He handed her a folded note.

Hally stared at it. She frowned. "What gentleman—" But the waiter was already heading back toward the bar.

Gord's brother watched her curiously, and Hally smiled and shrugged her shoulders. She opened the note.

Meet me on the balcony off the piano room.

It was signed: *B.A.*

Ben Atkinson.

Hally folded the note, and rose from her chair.

"Not bad news, I hope," said the young man beside her.

"I don't know," muttered Hally. She excused herself and wended her way past the head table.

Serina Heineault beckoned to her.

"So is this wedding giving you any ideas, Hally?" Her red lips shot up into a broad smile. "Ready to give up the single life, yet?"

Rudy guffawed and let out a good-humored groan. "Enjoy your single years while you can, Hally! I tried to warn Marla: 'Everything goes downhill right after the proverbial 'I do,' I told her. But would she listen?"

"I think you've had enough champagne, mister," said Serina, eyeing her husband with a chastising smile.

"Of course, if you find the right person to share your life with—" He grinned, and kissed Serina. She laughed and pretended to swat him away.

Hally left them, and paused at the bar. She called over the waiter who'd given her the note, and asked for directions to the piano room.

There was a man with silver hair and a neatly trimmed goatee playing a grand piano. A middle-aged woman sat next to him, swaying to the music, her eyes closed, a drink in her hand. The piano player nodded to Hally, singing in a gentle, rolling voice.

Hally passed the only other customers, a young couple who were too engrossed in each other to notice her. She stepped through the glass doors leading to the balcony.

The chilly November night air burst around her, but Hally welcomed it. She tilted her face toward the breeze and let the cold sweep away the heat in her cheeks.

"About time. Another ten minutes, and you'd be talking to an icicle," said a voice to her left.

Hally turned to the man standing in the shadows.

"My Mystery Man," she murmured, but loud enough for him to hear. *You've drunk too much champagne,* she scolded herself.

Ben stepped into the light. He was wearing a tuxedo,

and Hally was a little taken aback by how tall he appeared, how broad his shoulders were. His face had a chiseled look in the moonlight, and his eyes were deep and unfathomable as they gazed at her.

"You look beautiful, Hally."

"I look like a pink meringue."

"We haven't covered desserts, yet." He grinned. "But I wouldn't mind creating one that looks like you."

Hally could feel herself blush, and she gazed down at her hands awkwardly.

"What are you doing out here? Why don't you come into the reception?" She was talking fast, nervously. "They're just about to serve dessert. You didn't miss anything at dinner. You could use the squab as a spare tire, it was so tough. But then, I guess I've gotten used to using those big butcher knives of Lou Jay's—"

Ben squeezed her shoulders, looked down into her champagne-glittery eyes, and kissed her. Hally felt herself responding, her lips seeking out his as if they'd done this a million times before. But when he drew her in closer, she suddenly broke away.

"What do you think you're doing?" Her heart was hammering so hard, she could barely hear her own words.

"Reflex." Ben shrugged, his eyes not leaving her face. "You just looked so sweet in that dress, I couldn't help myself," he said unapologetically.

"So, that's why you dragged me out here, to—to—" She thrust her chin forward. "To kiss me?"

"I didn't drag you out here."

"You—you . . ." She tried to clear her head. Her lips felt as though they were on fire.

"You free tomorrow? I thought I'd take you skating. Since you broke our date, I figure you owe me."

"Owe you?" She shivered.

"You're cold." He slid off his tuxedo jacket. "Here," and he draped his coat about her shoulders.

"I'm not cold." But she didn't shrug off the jacket. "What are you doing out here, anyway? Why don't you come inside?"

"Something, er, came up at the last minute. I couldn't get a hold of you. I guess you were already at the church."

"Does this 'something' have to do with Veronica Wilmott?" Hally blurted out before she could stop herself.

Ben cocked an eyebrow, a glint of amusement dancing in his eyes. "Do I detect a note of jealousy?"

"Me? Jealous? Of whom? We hardly know each other!"

"Exactly. That's why I think we should go skating tomorrow."

"So I can see how well you crosscut and do figure eights? No, thank you."

"Don't tell me this beautiful advertising executive can't skate."

"I can skate." *If I can remember how*, she added to herself with a grimace.

"Fine. I'll pick you up—"

"I'll meet you," she interrupted.

"Have it your way." He sighed resignedly. "My, er, car's still in the shop, anyway. Walnut Arena. Two o'clock?"

"Make it two-thirty."

Ben smiled and chuckled, as if to himself. "You call the shots, Hally. Two-thirty it is."

Hally turned to leave, then glanced back at him. "You're—staying out here?"

Ben laced his hands behind his back. "I just need to cool off for a bit."

Hally shrugged and slid open the glass doors and didn't look back. She felt hot and jumpy. The squab roiled queasily in her stomach, and her head reeled, making her dizzy as she marched quickly past the still-swaying, and now swooning woman and the piano player. The silver-haired man's song followed her back to the reception like a shadow.

Hally sipped her coffee, staring at the tuxedo jacket draped across the sofa arm. After a moment, she got up and slid her hands into the pockets.

She recognized the rosebud in the left pocket as the one that had disappeared from her corsage. She glanced at the receipt. It was from a car rental agency. There was no signature. In his other pocket she found a business card: Walk-In Realtors. With it was a slip of paper that looked as though it had been torn from an envelope. Hally unfolded the paper and read it; it was her apartment address.

She guiltily returned the items into the jacket pockets, but found her hands lingering over the silk serge material. Expensive, she mused, her head buzzing still from the champagne. She smellt that heady, new-spring suede smell mingled with cigar smoke and a musky version of English Leather about the collar. After a moment Hally rose, her lids beginning to droop wearily as she hung Ben's jacket in the hall closet.

It looked strange hanging there, next to her long coat and jackets. But even as she shut the closet door, Hally became aware of its presence. Her heart suddenly careened forward, beating erratically against her ribs as the memory of Ben's kiss loomed back into her thoughts.

She'd enjoyed that kiss—too much, Hally thought, frowning. And though she was reluctant to admit it, she'd wanted him to kiss her as soon as she'd seen him there out on the patio.

Now, as she plodded into her bedroom and shed herself of the puffy, meringue-pink bridesmaid dress, Hally found she was no longer tired, but oddly restless. She needed to rein in her thoughts, regain her focus. She tugged on her flannel pajamas and reached for her briefcase. Spreading the contents of the Bel Abner file across her bed, she tugged on her earlobe and began to read.

Hally sat on the sofa sipping her morning coffee, gazing at the photos from the Bel Abner file. The press photos of Randall Abner depicted him as an unsmiling, severe-looking man with straight heavy brows, and a strong, slightly hooked nose. The mouth was full, but hidden beneath a neatly trimmed mustache and beard that immediately lent him an aristocratic appearance. The eyes peered at Hally warily. But behind the guarded expression was a keenness, a nervous kind of energy. He had the look of an observer, a man used to playing his cards strategically, and with meticulous thought and care.

An astute businessman, thought Hally, feeling already a little intimidated.

His wife, Deliah Abner, had a thoughtful, intelligent face, with expressive eyes and a mouth that curved naturally upward. Her chin and cheekbones were strong, and Hally gazed at the two of them posed side by side on an overstuffed sofa, and was struck by a sudden sense of recognition. There was something vaguely familiar about these people, she mused. But she couldn't quite nail it down to what—or who—these two people reminded her of.

She reread the highlighted portions from the *Business Biography Times*.

The Bel Abner Gourmet Company was founded by Belena and Wilhelm Abner, Randall Abner's Polish-German parents who emigrated to America in 1921. It was Belena's delicately beautiful face—a cross between Grace Kelly and Rosalind Russell—that still graced the labels of Bel Abner products.

Although originally based in Chicago, the Bel Abner Gourmet Company had swiftly begun to expand into the major metropolitan areas across the United States in the 1940s. Now they were successfully spreading into the Canadian and European markets. At one time, they were a delicious target for a Japanese takeover.

However, the company had managed to overcome obstacles and economic crises, as it had during the Depression and the competitive years following the Second World War, even managing to nudge out some of its major competitors. But their survival was mainly due to Belena Abner's astute business instincts concerning the stock exchange, along with her palpable charm and social influence. She became a favorite caricature in *New Yorkers Business Monthly,* a magazine read mostly by self-made entrepreneurs. Consequently, this exposure awarded Belena Abner, and Bel Abner Gourmet Products, a place on the Big Business map.

Three decades later, at the age of sixty-two, Belena Abner suddenly succumbed to pancreatic cancer, and died that same year. Four months later, her husband followed her. Reasons for his sudden death were never uncovered. Some had speculated (and it is still the consensus today) that Wilhelm Abner, being so devoted to his wife, had simply died of a broken heart.

Hally flipped through the clippings, and paused before the small article featuring Stewart Abner, the youngest son of Randall and Deliah Abner. There was a fuzzy headshot of the bespectacled man, his face turned slightly to the left. Hally frowned, squinting at the picture, trying to discern the features. But the photocopy was a poor one, and the wire-rimmed spectacles and the trim beard obscured the man's overall appearance. Yet she observed a passing resemblance to Randall Abner, though, too, there was something else about this man that seemed to strike a familiar chord in her.

In the article, she'd highlighted some passages referring to Benton Abner, the older brother. But Hally was surprised to find that Benton Abner was only thirty-five, a year older than she. She'd assumed the younger, bearded Stewart was nearing forty, at least. Hally read through the article, noting that he was married to Annabel Voisin, "... daughter of George Voisin of Voisin & Voisin Enterprises and—" Hally suddenly drew in a breath as she recognized the next name:

"—sister to model and television actress, Veronica Wilmott."

How had she missed *that* last night?

A knock on the door jarred her out of her reverie. She got up and answered it.

"Hi! Ready to go?" said Tina. "I'm double-parked. Garry took the kids skating, and I promised I'd be back after lunch."

"Oh, speaking of skating—" began Hally.

Tina poked her head in the doorway and peered around proudly. "By the way, you haven't told me what you think of the apartment so far. It's starting to take shape, don't you think?"

Hally nodded, trying to look enthusiastic. She opened the closet and reached for her jacket.

"What's this?" Tina fingered the sleeve of Ben's tuxedo. She raised an eyebrow. "I'm guessing you had a good time at the wedding. Did he leave last night or this morning?"

"Tina," Hally jerked an exasperated smile at her friend. "I, uh, just forgot to give it back to him last night."

"Him? Him who?"

Hally hesitated. "Ben Atkinson."

"The cooking partner? You invited him to the wedding?"

"Quit looking so smug. He-he didn't actually come to the wedding."

Tina gazed at her bemusedly.

"I met him—outside. On the balcony." Hally felt her cheeks beginning to burn.

"Hold it. Slow down. You met him on the balcony? Hmm... this sounds romantic." Tina's dark eyes gleamed. "Details. I want details."

"Well, you're not getting any. Nothing... important happened."

"Then why's your face all red?"

Hally swung her out the door. "Let's go. You're double-parked, remember?"

"Could it be true? Could Hally, Miss Career Woman I-Don't-Have-Time-for-Romance, actually be in love?"

"Let's not jump the gun," muttered Hally, slipping on her gloves. "But you'd better remind me to buy a pair of skates today." She ignored Tina's curious look, but found she could not suppress the smile that slowly crept across her face.

Hally lined up the bottles and plastic containers on the counter. Belena Abner's face winked at her, her smile stirring in Hally an odd sense of—what? Déjà vu? She scrutinized the woman again. There was definitely something familiar about the expression, the way the lips curved up, the brow—

"Well, of course she looks familiar, dummy," Hally berated herself aloud. "You've been staring at this stuff for over a week now." She sighed and gazed at the boxes of pots and pans. "This campaign is costing you a fortune," she told herself. "Now all you have to do is come up with a dinner plan—"

Plan. The skating rink! She'd almost forgotten about her date with Ben. She checked her watch: 2:10. Yes, she still had time. She stepped over the paint trays and stacked cans, and quickly donned her jacket. Scooping up her new pair of skates, Hally scooted out the door.

The crowd milled around her, and Hally had to push her way to the ticket booth. Parents chased after their kids, waving hats and mittens and skate guards. Hally stood on tiptoe scanning the length of the arena. She was ten minutes late, and the heavy traffic had murdered her good mood. A man in a Daniel Boone hat bumped into her, spilling coffee on her sleeve.

"Oh! I'm sorry, Miss. Here, let me help you."

Hally smiled through gritted teeth as he wiped at the sleeve of her jacket with a napkin. "Please, no. No, it's all right." She cast a sweeping glance behind him.

"You looking for somebody, Miss?" The man in the Daniel Boone hat smiled at her solicitously. "Listen, if you're looking for a skating partner—"

"She's got one, thanks," said a voice behind her.

Hally whirled around to face the man with the boyish grin and twinkling green eyes. He wore a bomber jacket, and slung casually over his shoulder were a pair of black hockey skates. Ben glanced at her skates, which she awkwardly held half-suspended in the air where the sharp toe picks couldn't jab her in the thigh. He grinned.

"You're late—as usual," Ben took her arm.

"You know, I'm never usually late. I hate being late, in fact. It's just recently I—"

"If you tell me you got stuck at work, I'll clobber you," he said, handing the man at the entrance gate two tickets. "For a moment I thought you were going to chicken out on me. I've been waiting here for over a half an hour."

"But I'm only a few minutes late," Hally said, consulting her watch. "You said two-thirty—"

"No, I said two. *You* said two-thirty."

"We agreed—"

The Gourmet Cupid 107

"Come on. There's only forty minutes left before they clear the ice." He grabbed her hand and led her past a group of overzealous parents and kids already garbed in their hockey gear, waiting to get onto the ice.

They sat on the benches and took off their boots. Hally shoved her feet into the stiff new skates, and began lacing them the way the clerk at the store had shown her.

"You might want to tie them a little looser," said Ben, watching her.

"I know how to lace up my skates, thank you," she retorted.

Ben continued to watch her, his head cocked slightly to one side, the corners of his mouth turned up in a half-bemused, amused smile. Hally could feel her face growing warm, conscious of his stare.

"What? What is it? Do I have something on my face?"

"I've just never seen you in jeans before. And your hair—it looks nice down like that." His grin turned wolfish. "Like you just got out of bed."

Hally's hand went to smooth her long blond tresses self-consciously.

"Ready?" Ben stood up, reached out a gloved hand for her arm, then pulled it back. "Sorry. I know how you like to do things on your own."

Hally's ankles wobbled in her new skates, the stiff leather making her feel like the Bride of Frankenstein learning how to walk all over again. She gripped the handrail and slowly followed Ben, who strode confidently down the steps.

What am I doing? she wailed to herself. *It's been years since I skated. But how hard could it be?*

She stepped onto the ice, gripping the boards. A young girl in a leotard whizzed past her, nudging her free arm and sending Hally flailing backward. Hally compressed her lips in concentration, her hold tightening on the boards. She was aware that Ben had turned around and was now waiting for her to catch up. Hally stroked and glided unsteadily on two feet. Darn it! This was harder than it looked.

"Warming up?" Ben stopped in front of her.

Sinatra was crooning from the arena speakers, and Ben hummed along with the melody as Hally performed another brave baby stroke. She balanced herself and glided forward. Encouraged, she took another stroke, but leaned a little too far to the left and teetered, her hand instinctively reaching for Ben's.

He righted her and clasped her hand tightly. "Been a while, has it?" His green eyes sought out hers, crinkling at the corners.

Hally managed a humble grin. "Don't worry. It'll come back to me." But she didn't let go of his hand.

Ben grinned. "Oh, I'm not worried."

They skated together—or rather, Ben skated, while Hally glided with him, taking intermittent tentative steps. Her ankles ached, and the leather at the top of her skates dug painfully into the bottoms of her calves. But she ignored this, more concerned for the moment about maintaining her balance. A group of youths slalomed around them at great speed, and their erratic momentum distracted Hally. She felt herself suddenly falling backward, and her legs skidded up as she flailed clumsily, trying to keep herself from falling. Her hand struck Ben in the face, and she crashed to the ice.

"Oopsy daisy," Ben helped her to her feet, laughing. "Yup. You're getting the hang of it, all right."

Hally shot him a black look. She wiped the snowy ice from her jeans, too angry and frustrated at herself to feel embarrassed. A couple zipped by them, followed by their progeny, three children who barely reached the height of her waist. They skated effortlessly past them, laughing, cheeks rosy, eyes sparkling. One of them moved to the center and began spinning. An old man stroked evenly around them, whistling between his teeth.

Hally forced herself onward. But her toe pick caught the ice, catapulting her forward. Ben gripped her arm and steadied her before she could fall.

"Hey, we're not in any hurry," he said, slipping his gloved fingers into hers. She resisted, trying to pull her hand away, but he only squeezed tighter. "Relax. Lean on me. You don't always have to be in control, you know."

Around you, I do, she replied silently.

As the music segued into "Embraceable You," a teenager, being chased by his friend, suddenly swerved in between Ben and the boards, and clipped him on the shoulder. Ben careened sideways against Hally, and they toppled like two dominoes, Ben landing on top of Hally. She blinked at him, momentarily startled by their proximity.

"I think we should stay right here," he said with a small groan.

Hally laughed. "What are you groaning about? Look who cushioned your fall."

He pulled her up with him. "You all right? No bones broken, I hope."

"Not yet, anyway." She sighed.

"Well, we've almost made it all the way round." He laughed, pointing across the rink to where they'd started.

"We can do it." Hally grinned.

The old man glided past them, still whistling cheerfully. Hally and Ben glanced at each other.

"I guess this just isn't my sport," confessed Hally, taking his hand.

"No, slicing and dicing seems to be more your forte," said Ben, nodding. "What do you like to do—besides learn gourmet cooking?"

Hally shrugged. "I don't know. I spend most of my

time working. I really don't have time for anything else.''

"How about movies?"

"I've been to one."

"Hmm ... well, would you like see another one?"

"With you?"

"No, with my chauffeur. Yes, of course with me."

"You have a chauffeur?"

Ben looked suddenly uncomfortable. "Sometimes," he replied, chewing on his lip.

Hally gazed at Ben, intrigued. This sudden turn of the conversation toward him interested her, and she quickly snatched up the opportunity before it managed to slip by.

"What do you like to do, Ben, besides skate and cook gourmet meals?" *Tell me about your father's company,* she added silently.

He mulled over this question for a long moment as they glided slowly along the ice.

"There was a time when I wanted to be a woodworker," he said. "You know, build things with my hands. But then I went off to college, and—well, one thing lead to another." His smile was grim. "And here I am."

Hally gave him a frustrated glare. "You're a man of few details," she said. "When you say 'here I am,' does that mean you're working now for your father's business?"

"Family business," he amended. "My mother wouldn't like to hear you say otherwise."

"And this family business," prompted Hally, "has you doing what, exactly?"

Ben glanced at her. "I can't tell you just yet, Hally."

Hally was startled by his honesty. "Why not? What's the big secret?"

"I just can't. Trust me on this."

The Gourmet Cupid 111

Hally frowned. Was Ben's family involved in something illegal?

And as if reading her thoughts, he quickly added, "It's nothing sensational or seamy, or anything like that."

Well, then why can't you tell me? wondered Hally, suddenly suspicious.

"Ah! Here we are. We made it in one piece," he said, stopping at the boards. "Back where we started."

"You're telling me," grumbled Hally.

"How're your feet holding up in those new skates?"

Hally grimaced. "You knew all along." She sucked air between her teeth. "I just bought them today, in fact. I think my ankles are on fire. As for my toes, I think they've melted into the leather. I can't feel them at all."

"Come on. I think I've put you through enough pain— for today, at least."

And tomorrow? wondered Hally.

"Tonight, I'll just take you to a nice movie where you don't have to do anything but sit and enjoy yourself," he said, swinging open the board gate.

"Tonight? Uh, I have some work I have to—"

"Take the night off."

"I can't. It's this, uh, campaign I'm working on," said Hally. "It-it's kind of important. Rain check?"

Ben eyed her, seeming about to say something, but stopped himself. "I'm holding you to it."

I'm glad, Hally found herself answering in silence. Her heart was thrumming contentedly as they climbed up the cement stairs.

They sat down and began unlacing their skates. Hally rubbed her ankles and toes, and reached underneath for her boots.

"Where—?" She rose from the bench and squatted down, searching for her boots. They weren't there.

Ben slid his feet into his, and looked over at her. "What's wrong?"

"My boots. Uh, they seem to be—" She scanned the length of the bench. "—gone."

Ben rose and hunkered down next to her. "Brown leather with white fleece, right?" He strode down along the adjacent bench and peered underneath.

"Hmm . . . looks like somebody made off with your boots."

"I can't go home in sock feet!" she wailed. She eyed the skates, rubbing her toes. "And I am *not* putting those back on!" Her socks were already sopping up the melted slush from the arena floor.

"Well, then, there's only one thing left to do." And before Hally could protest, Ben scooped her up in his arms. He grinned at her. "Off to the Lost and Found!"

Chapter Seven

"You can put me down now," said Hally tartly.

Ben glanced down at the uncarpeted floor of the apartment building. "I don't know. It looks awfully dirty. Maybe I'd better carry you up to your apartment."

"I'm fine." Hally sighed. "These socks can't get any dirtier."

Ben shook his head. "Uh-uh. I'm the one responsible for getting you into this mess. The least I can do is get you safely to your apartment."

"It's not your fault someone stole my boots, Sir Lancelot, or that the Walnut Arena doesn't have a lost and found." Hally struggled in his arms, but Ben held her firmly. "Whoever heard of an ice arena not having a lost and found?" she said grumpily.

"What floor?"

Hally let out a surrendering sigh. "Second. Take the stairs. Trust me, it's faster."

He grunted a little under her weight, but managed the stairs without complaint. Hally tried not to let the musky, new-spring suede smell of him overpower her, but nonetheless, she couldn't help relaxing against him, enjoying his warm breath in her hair, and the hard muscle of his arm beneath her thighs. Something tugged at her behind her ribs, and an inner warmth was slowly curling and tingling in the pit of her stomach.

"Number fourteen," he announced, pausing before her apartment door.

"Thanks."

He stared at the door.

"Okay, you can put me down now."

Ben gazed at her, considering her request, and for an instant Hally thought he wasn't going to let her down. But then, he gently lowered her legs to the floor, and Hally let go of his neck. She waited, smiling.

"You're not going in?" he asked, after a moment.

"You have my keys."

"Oh, right." He fished her keys out of his pocket. Hally opened the door, hesitating. Should she invite him inside? She was feeling strangely light-headed, and her heart was performing tricks, pumping too fast for her to think straight.

"Can I come in? I have to call a cab," he said.

"Yes. Yes, of course."

She'd forgotten about Tina's redecorating, and winced at the dissarray of the apartment. "It, uh, doesn't normally look like this," she apologized, pushing a paint tray to the side.

Ben had already taken off his boots, and his brows shot up as he gazed about the apartment. "It's certainly not what I expected," he said.

"My friend, Tina, she's fixing up my place for—" She paused. Ben looked at her. "For company," she finished.

"Must be important company," muttered Ben. He avoided the paint cans and strode past her, slipping off his gloves. "Whew! This November weather's given me a chill. I sure could use a nice hot cup of coffee right about now." He grinned at this not-so-subtle hint.

"How about some nice hot chicken stock?" suggested Hally.

"You made some chicken stock?"

Hally sighed. "I would have, but I didn't have time. How about some coffee, instead?"

Ben gave her a sidelong look. "Gee, what a novel idea."

Hally turned toward the kitchen. *What is wrong with you?* she chided herself. *Why are you acting so nervous?* She paused midway toward the kitchen, realizing she was still wearing her jacket. She unbuttoned it, and opened the hall closet. Her eyes darted immediately to the tuxedo jacket, and she could feel her temperature suddenly rise.

"I, uh, forgot. I have your tuxedo jacket here." Ben had moved next to her, and he followed her gaze.

"So you do," he said, his face close to hers.

Hally stepped back. "I tried to find you last night, after—" *After you kissed me,* she'd been about to say. "I'll make some coffee," she stammered, maneuvering around him.

Ben observed her, seemingly amused by her nervousness—which only made Hally all the more nervous. He watched her fumble in the kitchen for a moment, then proceeded to stroll across the canvas tarp into her living room. He cast a sweeping gaze over her bookshelves, pausing to inspect a miniature sculpture replica of the Iron Block Building.

"I remember doing a paper on Eero Saarinen. I liked him. He was more interesting than the other architects—quite eccentric."

"Oh?" said Hally from the kitchen. "You studied architecture at, uh—"

"The University of Iowa," Ben filled in for her. He shook his head and placed the sculpture back on the shelf. "Actually, I majored in French. I studied Spanish and Greek, too. Who knows why—" He emitted a low laugh. "Well, the truth is, I was in love with this girl—*thought* I was in love with her, anyway. And she was this kind of punker-beatnik type. She wanted to save the world from neoconservatism. I fell in love with her, and followed her to Iowa." Ben laughed. "My father nearly had a stroke when I told him I wasn't going to Yale." He laid his coat on the arm of the couch and peered down at the open file on the coffee table. He began to read, brows drawn together.

"So what happened to this girl?" asked Hally, pouring the coffee. "Uh, I hope you like instant."

Ben rifled through the clippings. "Lilith? Oh, she married a shoe salesman. The last I heard, they were living somewhere in Virginia."

Hally emerged from the kitchen bearing two mugs of coffee. As she handed him his coffee, she glanced down at the open file. Immediately she snatched it up, the contents spilling onto the paint canvas. Ben bent down to collect the newspaper clippings. Hally glared him.

"Do you mind? This is private business." She yanked the papers out of his hands.

"Sorry. I didn't mean to snoop," he said with an apologetic smile. "This the important campaign you're working on?"

Hally didn't answer. She slid the file safely back in her briefcase.

"Okay. I'm sorry. It's top secret, is it?" He sipped his coffee, regarding her over the rim of the mug. "So where'd you go to school? Here in Milwaukee?"

Hally eyed the couch, her momentary anger now replaced by that strange fluttering in her chest and stomach. Her pulse quickened, and her hands had suddenly turned cold and clammy. She gripped the coffee mug between her palms and sat down at the opposite end of the couch.

"Milwaukee? No, I studied at Notre Dame," she replied, staring, as if mesmerized, by the blond creamer swirls in her coffee. "I grew up in Indianapolis."

"Ah, yes. The 'Cinderella City,' " said Ben. "I should have known."

Hally gazed at him. "Why do you say that?"

"You seem to have a problem with losing shoes." He grinned.

"But I have a feeling my prince won't be coming to return them," grumbled Hally, wiggling her toes. She could feel blisters already forming at the backs of her heels.

"Well, you never know," said Ben cryptically. He set down his coffee, and gazed at her. "Wait a second. You have something in your hair—" He leaned over and put his fingers in her long blond tresses.

Hally stopped breathing, rooted to her spot on the couch. The musky outdoor smell of him mingled with his hot breath on her cheek. Her mind fogged with the sensation of his touch.

"Here it is." He showed her the tiny dried leaf. But he didn't move away. His gaze seemed to penetrate the depths of her amber-colored eyes, challenging them. Hally could not make herself look away. As his face came nearer, her eyelids fluttered closed.

He kissed her nose lightly, then brushed his lips along her cheek, trailing along the curve of her cheekbone down to her chin. A small gasp rose in Hally's throat as his mouth finally claimed hers. His lips pressed gently at first, then grew more insistent. Hally's lips responded, and he clasped her shoulders, drawing her to him. Instinctively, her arms entwined about his neck, and his fingers caressed her back, entangling passionately in her hair.

"Hally." He nibbled her earlobe, and kissed her throat. "You drive me crazy," he rasped.

You drive me *crazy,* Hally's thoughts reeled back. Her hands traced the hardness of his shoulders, feeling the muscles of his biceps grow taut under the touch of her exploring fingers.

The knock at the door startled them, and Hally's

abrupt movement sent her coffee mug tumbling off the table.

For a moment, they both stared at the brown liquid running down into the creases of the paint canvas.

Hally leapt to her feet, blinking her thoughts back into focus. She bounded into the kitchen as the person at the door knocked again.

"Hally?" came a muffled voice. "You home?"

Hally winced: Tina. She hesitated between the kitchen and the door.

"I'll get it," said Ben, rising. And before Hally could protest, he was opening the door.

"... I forgot my key—oh! Hello." Tina gazed at Ben in surprise.

Hally ducked into the kitchen, running a quick hand through her mussed hair, and straightened her sweater. She grabbed the tea towel off the oven rail and came out just as Ben was introducing himself.

"Oh, you're Hally's cooking partner," said Tina.

Ben glanced around at Hally, his eyebrows lifting slightly. "Hally mentioned me, did she?"

Hally flushed, and was furious at herself for doing so. She shot a quick warning look at Tina and went into the living room to sop up the spilled coffee.

"Good thing I covered the rug," said Tina, watching Hally. "I didn't—" She glanced over at Ben. "—interrupt anything, did I?"

Hally looked up sharply. "No. Ben was just about to leave. Isn't that right?"

"Right." Ben nodded. "Where's the phone? I have to call a taxi."

Tina directed him to the kitchen. She hunkered down next to Hally, her expression lit with wonder. "Hally! He's gorgeous!" she whispered enthusiastically. "Were you two—? You know, I could leave if you want—"

"Tina, please don't embarrass—"

The Gourmet Cupid 119

Ben came out of the kitchen. He ran a quick hand over the back of his hair and grinned easily at them. "Cab'll be here in a few minutes. Milwaukee has great transit service."

Tina tilted her head inquiringly. "Oh, then you're not from Milwaukee, Mr. Atkinson?"

"Chicago, actually." He glanced at Hally. "But I've been seriously thinking of moving here."

Hally recalled the realty card she'd found in his tuxedo pocket. *The Kingsdale Hotel: that must be where he's staying,* thought Hally. She glared at the back of his head.

"Well, Mr. Atkinson—" began Tina.

"Please, call me Ben."

"Ben, is that short for Benedict? Or—"

"It's just . . . Ben."

"Well, Ben, seeing that you're a visitor to this city, I don't suppose you have plans for Thanksgiving? Because you're welcome to join us. It'll just be my husband and I and the twins—and Hally, of course."

Ben grinned at Hally. "Well, that's awfully nice of you, Tina. I'd love to come for Thanksgiving dinner."

Hally's stomach turned over.

But before Tina could ply Ben with any more questions, he smiled politely, "I really should be going. I've already had three cab drivers leave on me this week." He turned to Hally. "Sorry about your boots, Cinderella. But you never know—your prince might come along sooner than you think." He winked at her.

Hally and Tina watched him leave.

"I *did* interrupt something," said Tina, narrowing her eyes curiously. "So what was that all about? Boots—?"

Hally shook his head. "Don't ask."

Tina tittered. "Okay, Cinderella."

Hally winced, and glanced down at her soiled, damp socks. She would have to go buy another pair of boots—

and another pair of socks. It wouldn't do to be wearing dirty socks if her prince did happen to show up.

Hally awoke, shivering. The tip of her nose was numb with cold, and she snuggled back down into the warmth of her bedcovers. The snooze alarm beeped again insistently, and she shut it off, reluctantly climbing out from her nice warm nest. She slipped into her terrycloth robe and went into the kitchen to call the landlord about the heat.

The line was busy. As she hung up, Hally's gaze shifted into the dining room, toward the balcony window.

The railing and her deck chairs had vanished beneath a blanket of white. An undulating pattern of crystallized ice decorated the glass patio doors. Flakes of snow, like powdered sugar, sprinkled down steadily across the blue. Hally groaned and tramped into the kitchen to make some coffee.

Showered, dressed, and ready to attack the oncoming workday, Hally opened the closet. Darn it! Ben had forgotten to take his tuxedo jacket. She pulled it free of the hanger. She'd return it to him tonight at the gourmet class. But the thought of seeing him again sent her heart skipping. And yet, at the same time, something tightened in the pit of her stomach.

What are you doing, Hally? she scolded herself. *You can't be falling in love—not now. You're a career woman; work must come first.*

With a determined grimace, she opened the door and nearly tripped over a package perched upon her welcome mat.

Curious, she reached for it, and gazed at the familiar scrawl on the front: *For Cinderella.*

She shook the package, but had already guessed its contents; and she didn't have to guess who had sent it.

"My prince has come," she murmured, not knowing whether to be happy, angry, or frustrated. In the end, when she saw how perfectly the boots fit, she was happy and angry—and frustrated.

Hally drove to Humboldt Lodge, trying to keep her thoughts on the Bel Abner campaign. Luckily, Danny and Marla were working at peak performance today. With the wedding now behind her, and having her honeymoon to look forward to, Marla seemed more focused than ever. But Hally had found her mind meandering all day, unable to concentrate, daydreaming during the meetings, having to pinch herself to keep Ben Atkinson from drifting into her thoughts.

Yet, there was still something about him that continued to gnaw at her—a missing piece she couldn't seem to grasp. And she knew it was right there on the cusp of her thoughts, waiting to be uncovered.

Ben sat on the couch, talking with Charles and his mousy partner. Hovering nearby was the keen-eyed journalist, Karl MacAvoy. He observed Ben thoughtfully, but when he looked up and saw Hally entering the room, he quickly left his perch and strode over to her.

"Hello. Hally, isn't it?"

"Hi." She smiled uncertainly. "How's the, uh, article coming?"

"Great. Hally? Listen, can I ask you something?" His voice lowered to a hushed whisper as he steered her to the corner of the room. "How well do you know Ben Atkinson?"

Hally frowned. "Ben? I-I—" *I don't know him at all,* she answered silently. "Not very well, really. Why?"

"Has he told you about himself? I mean, where he's from? What he does for a living? About his family?"

"A little," she replied hesitantly. Why was this man so interested in Ben?

"You see," Karl went on, as if anticipating her question, "I suspect Ben Atkinson isn't really who he says he—"

"Hello there, partner!" Ben interrupted them. He nodded to Karl MacAvoy. His green eyes were flashing, and his smile revealed his even white teeth.

Like a warning signal, thought Hally. Or was that a sign of territoriality?

Ben's hand cupped her elbow. "If you don't mind, I'm going to steal my Gourmet Heart away from you for just a moment, Karl."

The journalist smiled uncertainly, but Hally was conscious of his swift observing eyes making mental notes as they excused themselves.

"I see the boots fit," he said in a low, conspiratorial voice that made Hally flush a little.

"Yes, they're, uh, very nice," she stammered. "I-I'd like to pay you back." She reached in her briefcase for her checkbook.

Ben stopped her. "They were a gift. It was the least I could do. Besides, when I saw them, they had Hally Chrisswell written all over them."

"They're Canadian leather. They're much too extravagant—"

"They'll last you a lifetime." His eyes devoured her, lingering for a long moment on her lips. His expression was oddly serious. "Speaking of which, guess who's getting married."

Hally's heart leaped up into her throat, and she almost gasped aloud. *Please, I don't even know you. Please, don't ask me to marry you—*

"Hally, hi." Charles stood up and looked to Ben. "Did you tell her yet?"

Ben shook his head, grinning.

"Now, wait a minute—" she began, flustered.

Charles put his arm around his mousy cooking partner,

who blushed to the roots of her hair. "Monique and I are engaged to be married."

Something popped inside Hally's chest, and the remainder of her personal integrity slowly leaked out. How could she have entertained such a preposterous idea as Ben asking her to marry him? If she'd been alone she would have laughed aloud at herself.

"Hally? Aren't you happy for us?" Monique touched her arm.

"Oh, hey! This is wonderful! Congratulations!" Hally shook their hands.

"Who would have thought two people could fall in love so quickly?" said Charles happily. He gazed at Hally and Ben. "Sometimes fate just steps in and throws you a curve, tossing the right two people together." He grinned. "Only you have to let down your guard long enough to see it."

Hally squirmed uncomfortably beneath the couple's gaze. Ben, too, appeared a little ill at ease, his usual poise all of a sudden faltering; Charles's words, they both suspected, were subtly directed toward them.

First Tina, now Charles and Monique. Hally sighed. What was it about her single status people felt the need to change? To fix? Couldn't they see she was happy being single? she thought angrily.

"Hey, what's got you upset all of a sudden?" Ben frowned at her, concerned.

"I'm not upset," she answered tersely. "I'm . . . very happy."

Lou Jay burst through the doorway behind them, his bulky frame filling the doorway. "Greetings, my student Gourmet Hearts! Please forgive my tardiness," he said, red-faced and wheezing. He dabbed his forehead with his chef's hat before he plopped it on his head.

"So much to do, so much to do." He shook his head with a long-drawn-out sigh. He clapped his hands, muttering, as if to himself: "Tonight we will be preparing *coulis de tomates aux poivrons rouge*—tomato and pepper coulis—and onion soup gratiné." He touched his lips in a kiss of sudden inspiration.

He resumed his place in the fluorescent limelight of the kitchen, and glanced at his students. "And this evening I will teach you the secret of the egg." He winked. "Now, what came first, do you think? The chicken or the egg?"

"First comes love, then comes marriage—" Ben whispered teasingly in her ear.

Hally's black look made him bite back the remainder of the song. She flipped open her notebook as Lou Jay delved into more philosophical culinary questions. Hally twirled her pen in her hand and shut her brain off. She didn't want to reflect on anything that might lead to more puzzling questions.

She snuck a quick glance at Ben, who was listening with amused attentiveness. The way he held his head, with his chin thrust forward, his lips turned slightly upward, the strong aristocraticlike profile—this man exuded a kind of confidence, poise, *mystery* that instinctively drew her to him.

No, thought Hally, with a shake of her head; it wouldn't do to get mixed up with this man; she already had enough mystery in her life, as it was.

Hally and Ben walked together out into the parking lot. They'd barely spoken to each other all night. Several times, Hally had turned to him, intending to say something to ease the tension that seemed to have risen all of a sudden between them. But it was as though she were trying to peer over a neighbor's hedge which was dividing the private property of their thoughts. She couldn't even guess what he was thinking.

But obviously, Sunday's episode was still fresh in

their minds. And for some reason that kiss in her apartment had managed to trigger this new atmosphere of awkwardness that both of them were trying unsuccessfully to ignore.

Did he regret kissing her? Hally wondered.

"Do you—" She cleared her throat. "Do you need a ride to the, uh . . . hotel?"

Ben chewed on his lip. "I should have told you I was staying there," he said, looking a little sheepish. "There's a lot of things I should tell you, in fact." He touched her arm, stopping her. "Hally, would you like to grab a coffee, or something?"

She really needed to go over the financial figures for the campaign tonight, she thought, eyeing her cooking partner. But a warm giddiness started up in the pit of her stomach as she glimpsed Ben's intent, imploring expression.

"Uh, yes," she heard herself reply. Her face broke out into a wide, generous smile. "Yes! Actually, I would like that very mu—"

"Yoo-hoo! Ben! Benny, darling!"

Hally and Ben whirled about on their heels and gazed in startlement at the woman who seemed to have appeared out of nowhere, and who was now standing and waving at them in front of a white limousine.

A black ermine mink stole draped itself across the woman's milky shoulders, and she posed, waspish-waisted, deep chestnut brown hair swept back from her face in a glamorous forties style. Hally immediately put together the beautiful face and the fabulous hourglass figure: Veronica Wilmott.

The expression on Ben's face was unreadable, but Hally thought she saw a momentary flicker of frustration twitch his lips. Michael had abandoned his cooking partner, and had rushed over to Veronica Wilmott, smoothing back his already slicked-back hair. But Karl

MacAvoy was already there, shoving his tiny tape recorder in the television actress's face.

Ben smiled ruefully at Hally. "Looks like my ride's here. Maybe we could—"

"I'll see you Wednesday," said Hally with a cold smile. She turned and strode deliberately toward her car.

As she nosed her Mustang out of the lot, she glimpsed Ben talking to Karl MacAvoy. The journalist looked puzzled and vaguely disappointed. Veronica Wilmott was frowning at Ben, as if confused by the men's conversation. Hally gazed at Ben through the front windshield, and for a moment his eyes locked onto hers. Hally averted her eyes and pressed her foot to the accelerator, speeding past the limousine. When she was safely en route back to her apartment, she gasped, realizing she'd been holding her breath.

Her stomach churned uneasily, and her hands were hot and sweaty as they gripped the steering wheel. She lowered the window, the cold November air a soothing balm on her flaming cheeks.

Ben and Veronica Wilmott. They were together: a couple. Was this what Ben wanted to tell her? That he was already involved with someone?

Her fingers went to her lips, still able to feel the sensual heat of his mouth, his hands caressing her back—

She braked hard as she nearly rammed into the back of the station wagon in front of her.

"Calm down, Hally," she scolded herself aloud. She draped her hand across her forehead as if to keep any further thoughts about Ben Atkinson from leaking out of her head.

"Remember, Hally, the Bel Abner campaign is due in less than three weeks." She smiled grimly at her reflection in the rearview mirror.

But a dull weight had already anchored itself in her chest, and her temples were aching from clenching her teeth. As she swerved onto 124th Street, her mind was suddenly perforated with images: Ben and Veronica Wilmott holding hands, dancing together, limbs entwined, Ben's lips trailing kisses along Veronica's porcelain throat, murmuring how much he loved her.

Hally swallowed back her nausea, but in the same instant, anger was also surging through her. She gripped the steering wheel tighter.

Her anger was directed toward Ben, yes—but she was more angry with herself. How could she have let him make such a fool of her? How could she have allowed herself to become so distracted by this man—a man she didn't even know?

And yet, the truth was all the more maddening. Hally was reluctant to admit it—for so long it had been since she'd let herself fall for a man—but yes, she thought with a sigh . . . she was jealous.

The red button on her answering machine was flashing, telling her she had five messages. Hally shuffled into the living room and slumped down wearily on her sofa. She gazed at the wall before her. Tina had replaced her old framed cat poster with a large Renoir print of a bearded man and a woman dancing. She noted Tina had rearranged her knickknacks, adding photographs of Hally and her family, along with a new black-and-white portrait of Hally gazing up at the Milwaukee Public Museum.

It was a good photograph of her, taken by Garry some years ago. But she'd found it disturbing, perhaps because the lens had caught her unaware, unprepared. It revealed a side of her, a vulnerability in her, Hally didn't often like to show.

Hally rose from the couch and stuffed the black-and-white photograph between two books. Tina was crossing a fine line with this redecorating, she mused disapprovingly. Her apartment seemed almost to be assuming a personality of its own. But more to the point, the newly painted walls and Tina's subtle flourishes were opening up a different side in Hally—and, much to her chagrin, Hally was finding herself beginning to enjoy her new surroundings.

She strode into the kitchen, navigating around the remaining paint cans and trays, and played her answering machine.

"Hi, it's me," said Tina. "Put that photograph back!" Hally sighed, rubbing her eyes. Tina had eyes at the back of her head.

"... be back tomorrow," Tina's voice went on. "I found this great fish border for your bathroom. And yes, it was on sale. So I'll see ya later—and tell your handsome *friend*" Tina emphasized the word "friend," "that he's expected here at six for Thanksgiving dinner. Okay?" Hally groaned.

"Don't work too hard, Hally.... Oh, by the way, I saw the absolutely most perfect dress for you at Geldorf's this morning. Ben will love it!" Hally could feel Tina winking through the machine. "But I saw another woman eyeing it—you know what? I think it was actually Veronica Wilmott! You know, the television star?"

Hally bared her teeth at the machine.

"Anyway, I thought I'd pick it up for you. I know how busy you are these days. We'll talk tomorrow after your cooking class."

Hally groaned. *Don't bother to pick up that dress. I have a feeling Ben's not coming for Thanksgiving dinner.*

The second beep sounded as she opened the refrigerator.

"Hally? Danny here. Some guy from the research department dropped off a package after you left. A magazine, I think. But you have to go up and sign for it. Something about a fine for a previous lost item?"

"Anyway." Danny coughed, and went on. "I just wanted to tell you I'm not coming in tomorrow. It seems my little one has come down with the chicken pox, and Susie is flying out to Chicago for some fashion convention. Apparently, Veronica Wilmott is supposed to be making a special appearance. Call me tomorrow at home if you need me, Hal."

Veronica Wilmott. Everywhere Hally turned, this woman seemed to be popping out of some aspect of her life.

Hally took a long gulp from the carton of milk and stared at the painting of the tomato. The cupid's eyes seemed to turn on her suddenly, and Hally raised her fingers, miming a gun, and pulled the trigger.

"I'll get you before you get me," she muttered.

Bee-ee-eep! "Hello? Hally?" A beat passed, and for a moment Hally's heart paused in its rhythm.

"Hmm... I guess you're not home yet. It's Ben, by the way. I just wanted to explain—" She heard him mutter a low curse. "Well, I'll call you later." There was a click.

Another beep rang in the air, and Hally's hand clutched the end of the counter.

"It's me again," said Ben. Hally heard him sigh. "I have to take off, but I'd really like to speak with you... Are you there? Pick up if you're there..." He waited. "Okay, so either you're not home, or you don't want to talk to me." Ben sighed. "I guess we'll see each other on Wednesday." A long pause. In the background Hally heard a woman's voice, beckoning to him: Veronica Wilmott's voice.

"I have to go," Ben said quickly. "I'll see you Wednesday."

Almost in the same breath, the final message beep hiccuped through the kitchen:

"By the way," said Ben, "should I bring anything for

Thanksgiving dinner?" And his call was cut off by a woman's whining: "Come on, honeybear. We're going to be late!"

Honeybear? Hally gagged at the machine.

"Till Wednesday," Ben's sultry whisper floated up from the answering machine.

Hally narrowed her eyes at the cherubic figure in the painting. Its empty bow laughed at her, and her gaze was drawn to the couple embracing in the privacy of the tomato leaves. Smiling triumphantly at her, the cupid's chorus echoed in the hallways of her mind:

> *Hally and Ben, sittin' in a tree,*
> *K-I-S-S-I-N-G!*
> *first comes love . . .*

Chapter Eight

"*Diable de mer:* the ugly monkfish." Lou Jay made an extravagant gesture at the fish sprawled across the cutting boards.

Hally and Ben exchanged wrinkled-nosed winces, but Charles and Monique, who had teamed up with them, seemed at the moment more interested in each other than the food.

Karl MacAvoy had attempted to squirm his way into partnering with Hally and Ben, but the chef had already organized his Gourmet Hearts into three separate groups. Michael had also protested, winking at Hally, trying to get her attention while he and the journalist and their partners prepared a braised chicken dish. The third group was cooking a New York strip steak with homemade *frites*.

"Naturally, we get stuck with the ugly fish," muttered Hally. Seafood didn't sit well with her, and here staring up at her with glassy, glazed eyes was indeed two of the ugliest fish she'd ever seen.

"Don't be fooled by their unfortunate appearance," said Lou Jay, resting his hand on Hally's shoulder. "These fellows offer us a rich, wonderful flavor beyond anything you could imagine." He kissed his lips with his fingers. "Your gums will absolutely melt," he assured them.

Hally gazed at the fish dubiously, running her tongue protectively over her teeth. She squinted at the recipe taped to the wall. "I think I'll, uh, help prepare the sauce."

"Sure, let the brave men handle the real stuff," said Ben, puffing out his chest. But Charles swayed a little, paling slightly as Ben handed him the filetting knife.

Hally popped the red bell peppers into the roaster and began chopping the fresh parsley.

"You're very good at this," said Monique, wielding her knife awkwardly. "I was wondering, are you a writer, or something? You seem to be taking a lot of notes."

"No." Hally smiled. "I'm in advertising, actually. I—I have to cook a meal for some... clients." *Potential clients,* she amended silently. But *diable de mer* wasn't exactly what she'd had in mind for the menu. The macédoine of seasonal vegetables she and Ben had prepared earlier was something she might be able to fit in as a first course, but somehow, too, Hally would have to incorporate the Bel Abner Gourmet products.

"Well, our men seem to be having fun." Monique gazed at Charles, a loving expression spreading across her thin face. "I wonder how Lou Jay knew?" She blushed suddenly. "I mean, pairing us up the way he did. You know what I mean. It's like Charles is the other half of my Gourmet Heart—just like Ben is yours."

Hally glanced up at her sharply. "Oh, Ben and I—"

"We'd love you and Ben to come to the wedding." She giggled shyly. "In a way, it was you two who brought us together."

"Oh?"

"Yes. The way you two look at each other." She sighed, gazing down at her knife dreamily. "Who knew love could be so contagious?"

Ben peered over Hally's shoulder. "You sure you don't want to help me with this fish, partner?"

Hally gave him a long look, and he winced, biting his

lower lip. Monique had already glided over to her fiancé, and was nuzzling her thin face in the crook of his arm.

"How long are you going to keep this up?" said Ben irritably. "You haven't said a word to me all night."

Hally continued to chop, though the parsley was beginning to mush itself into the cutting board, and the red pepper looked like a mound of tiny red ants.

"You're not even going to let me explain, are you?" said Ben. "Like I said before, Veronica Wilmott doesn't mean anything to me. She's—she's a friend of the family, that's all."

Hally glanced up at him briefly, considering his admission. Why should she trust him? She hardly knew anything about him.

"The thing is," Ben continued slowly, weighing his words carefully, "I'm leaving Milwaukee tonight."

Hally paused, waiting. His face was near hers, and his breath feathered gently against her cheek. She kept her eyes fixed to the chopping board, not daring to move, lest she suddenly fall into his arms. Oh, she wanted him to kiss her again—

"I really wanted to spend Thanksgiving with you, Hally, but—"

Hally's back went rigid. "Look, you don't have to feel obligated to come. If you made other plans—" *With Veronica Wilmott,* she almost said, but restrained herself.

"I'm, er, actually leaving the country. Ah, it's a family thing." He sighed. "It completely slipped my mind. I guess I got a little . . . sidetracked." His grin was smug and rueful at the same time. "I think I need to clear up some things before I—"

"Mr. Atkinson?" Lou Jay interrupted them. "There is a woman asking for you at the door."

Both Hally and Ben gazed behind them at the sylphlike figure leaning against the doorframe. Veronica Wilmott waved a black gloved hand, the other poised delicately on her hip. She tossed back her gleaming chestnut hair and preened, her body beckoning to Ben: "Come here, you big handsome boy."

Ben glanced down at his watch and grimaced. Guilt rode across his features, and as Hally glanced at him, he looked for an instant like a schoolboy caught staying out after curfew. He turned to her uncertainly.

"This isn't what it looks like. Veronica's flying over with me, yes, but—"

"You don't have to explain. Have a good trip."

"I wish I had more time." Ben rubbed his face. "I know what you're thinking—"

"You don't know what I'm thinking."

"Yes I do. And it's wrong what you're thinking; you have it all wrong."

"Thanks for clearing that up. I feel so much better."

"If you'd only let me explain—" He let out a frustrated groan. "I should have told you the truth from the beginning—"

"Well, now I know the truth."

"But you don't. Hally, listen, can I call you?"

Veronica Wilmott waved again, accompanied by a not so subtle: "Ho-oneybear! We're going to be late for our flight!"

"Your girlfriend beckons," said Hally curtly, returning to her mushy parsley and finely chopped red pepper.

Ben sighed. "Okay, okay—so we were engaged briefly. But that was a long time ago—"

"The plot thickens," Hally interrupted him. "But to tell you the truth, I don't have time for all this cloak-and-dagger stuff. My life is complicated as it is."

"I don't want to complicate your life. It's just that—"

"You'd better go, or you'll miss your flight," said Hally frostily, not meeting his eyes.

"I'm sorry about the class—leaving you like this in the middle—"

"It's not the middle; it's the end. Have a nice trip—to wherever you're going."

"Gee, if you'd just let me explain—"

Hally forced a smile on her face. "Really, there's no need, Mr. Atkinson. I understand perfectly. No harm done. If you're ever in the neighborhood, give me a ring." Her words flew off her tongue as if divorced from her brain. She managed to maintain eye contact, her face strangely calm and composed.

Charles stepped toward them. "Uh, Ben? You ready to steam the fish?" He glanced at him, then over at Hally, and frowned. He cleared his throat and adjusted his thick spectacles. "Is, uh, anything wrong?"

Hally broke free of Ben's gaze. "Wrong? No, nothing's wrong," she said with forced cheeriness.

Ben told Charles that he had to leave, that he wouldn't be coming to any more classes.

Monique, overhearing this, glanced at Hally, stricken. "You mean, you two are leaving us?"

Ben fished a pen from his pocket and wrote down the number for the Kingsdale Hotel on a receipt stub. "If you want to get a hold of me, leave a message at the hotel, and I'll try to get back to you." His green eyes shifted to Hally. "The wedding's next month, isn't it?"

"December seventeenth, but where—?"

"Don't worry. I'll be back before then," Ben assured Charles. He hesitated before starting toward the door, and flashed a quick grin at Hally. "See you later . . . my Gourmet Heart," he muttered gently.

They watched him leave, with Veronica Wilmott leaning her head against Ben's shoulder, linking her arm comfortably with his.

"Who's that woman? She looks awfully familiar," said Charles to no one in particular.

"Isn't she—?" began Monique.

"Veronica Wilmott." Hally nodded.

Charles removed his spectacles and proceeded to clean them. "You mean the television actress? What's Ben doing with someone like her?"

Monique elbowed her fiancé, shooting him a disapproving look, gesturing faintly in Hally's direction.

"She's not really so pretty," said Charles quickly.

Yes she is, replied Hally silently. A ball of misery was bouncing inside the cavity of her chest.

"One shouldn't be fooled by appearances," Monique spoke out, glancing over at the filleted *diables de mer*. "And, besides, it's obvious she doesn't have a Gourmet Heart," she declared, her usual timid voice suddenly full of assurance.

Hally gazed at the mousy woman standing next to her, arms uncharacteristically folded across her chest, a knowing—almost haughty—expression on her thin face.

Gourmet Heart? thought Hally, sneering. She rolled her eyes. *Who needs a Gourmet Heart?*

"I don't know what's wrong with me," said Hally. "All of a sudden I'm so restless. I can't concentrate at work. Everything seems to annoy me. People are irritating me for practically no reason." She tugged hard at her earlobe, wincing. "I nearly ran over a pedestrian this morning because he was taking too long crossing the crosswalk—and he was on crutches!"

Hally rose from Tina's ottoman and paced about the room. "Marla brought in her wedding photos today, and I proceeded to cut up every one of them. And I'm telling you, they weren't that bad! Poor Marla was practically in tears by the time she left the office this evening." She pressed the heel of her palms against her eyes, moaning in frustration. "Oh, I am such a horrible person."

Tina eyed her friend, said nothing for a moment, then sat back against the couch, regarding her with an

The Gourmet Cupid   137

amused, tranquil smile. "You're not a horrible person, Hally. You're just in love."

"Oh, no. Don't start that." Hally waggled her finger at her. "I'm a nutcase, that's what I am. I'm cracking under pressure. What exactly have I learned in that stupid gourmet class, anyway?"

"I thought you already put together a menu?"

Hally closed her eyes. "I did, I did. But how am I going to cook it? I can't cook!"

"Sure you can. You've been doing it for over three weeks now." Tina cocked her head, her eyebrows raising slightly. "Or is it that you can't cook without Ben Atkinson?"

"I've been cooking for the past week and a half without him." *The jerk*, she added to herself; he hadn't even called her. But then, it wasn't exactly as if she'd given Ben an open invitation. And he was out of the country—

"Hally, you are so stubborn. Why can't you just admit that you fell for Ben Atkinson?" Tina opened her palms as if offering her friend a gift. "And why not? He's really quite handsome. He's obviously not hurting for money, and the way he looked at you—"

"I'm not in love with him!" But her own protest sounded weak and unconvincing. She gazed at Tina, irritated. "And I hardly know him. Besides, he's seeing Veronica Wilmott."

"I thought he said she was just a friend of the family."

"They were once engaged to be married." Hally shook her head. "I don't know. There's something about him. . . . Do you know I still don't have a clue what business his family is in?"

"You mean, you think he's involved in something . . . illegal?"

"I don't know. But he was certainly secretive about it." Hally sighed. "In any case, I have the Bel Abner presentation next week." She snapped her fingers, grimacing. "Which reminds me. I've been so busy I forgot to pick up that stupid magazine from the research department. Ah! What does it matter now? Danny and Marla have come up with a great campaign idea—well, I suppose it was *partly* my idea." She recalled that afternoon as the three of them sat in the office, batting ideas back and forth. And somehow the conversation had turned to cooking...

"Gourmet Heart?" Marla had repeated, looking thoughtful. "Hally, I think you might be on to something."

Hally suddenly realized her mistake. "No, wait—"

But sparks were already flying from Danny's eyes. "It's brilliant!" he said excitedly. "The concept is certainly corny enough. And as we all know, the cornier the romance, the better it sells."

And, indeed, the comps and concept sketches they'd come up with were brilliant and original, and just "corny" enough to appeal to any American consumer with but a smidgen of romance in his heart. And, as Danny had so succinctly put it: "Everyone has fallen in love at least once in their lifetime."

"This campaign sounds terrific, Hally," said Tina.

Hally massaged her temples. "But now, with Danny having to go to Green Bay for his kid's hockey tournament, and Marla leaving for Jamaica on her honeymoon—"

"So you'll do it alone. I know you'll do great, Hally," Tina reassured her. "At least the apartment's finished."

Rory and Gloria came bounding into the living room, and Rory hid behind Hally, nearly knocking her over.

Tina furrowed her brow. "Gloria! Stop chasing your brother!"

"He started it!"

Rory pulled on Hally's pant leg. "I'm hungry!"

Tina sidestepped a toy dump truck. "I'll make dinner in a minute. Pick up these toys, please. You want Aunt Hally to break her neck?" Tina's eyes suddenly lit up. "Oh, I didn't tell you! I got a decorating job! Roger Chetner just got a promotion, you see, and Garry told Roger about my decorating your apartment, and so he asked me if I'd decorate *his* new office."

"Hey, that was nice of him."

Tina rolled her lip between her teeth. "Um, yes. He told me to say 'hi,' and to say he'll see you at Thanksgiving."

"Thanksgiving?"

"Yes. Didn't I tell you? It looks like he'll be able to make it, after all. Isn't that great?"

Hally groaned loudly.

"See? You don't have to be so glum," said Tina cheerfully. "Everything worked out in the end."

Except that the wrong person was coming for dinner, thought Hally gloomily.

"You have to leave already?" said Roger, rising.

Hally stifled a yawn. Her head was a snow globe blurring with interest percentages, probability statistics, and rising insurance rates. "Unfortunately, duty calls," she said with a polite smile.

"Hmm . . . yes. I understand." Roger nodded soberly. He ignored Rory, who was trying to show him his Elmo doll. "I should be heading out, as well. Do you need a ride home?"

This time, Hally'd had the foresight to arrive at Tina's in her own car. "Thanks, but no. My Mustang's parked outside." She turned to Tina and Garry, who'd been strangely quiet the entire evening. She thanked them for the dinner.

Roger shook Garry's hand, and kissed Tina's cheek. "Yes, the meal was incredible, Tina. It almost makes me want to chuck all this crazy career business of mine, and start up a family of my own." He laughed. Rory tugged on his pantleg, and he shrugged the twin off.

Tina gave Hally a sidelong look, her brows raised. "Well, when the right person comes along—" She linked her arm in Garry's and rested her head contentedly on her husband's shoulder. "—you have to grab him before it's too late."

Garry grinned at her. "Yep. As soon as this one got her hooks in me, I was a goner."

"Actually, Garry pursued me. I just let him catch me," teased Tina. "I was just honest enough with myself to see he was the right man for me."

Hally winced; these last words, she knew, were for her benefit. She bent down and hugged Gloria, who rested her small curly head on her shoulder, yawning. Rory pulled at the sleeve of her coat and held up Elmo.

"He can sleep over at your house, if you want, Aunt Hally," said Rory. "So you won't have to be alone."

Hally regarded Elmo's fuzzy red body, and smiled awkwardly at the twin. She avoided Tina's amused look. "Well, thanks, Rory, but I think Elmo would rather hang out with you tonight. Besides, he'd get homesick at my apartment."

Roger gazed at the stuffed animal, wrinkling his brow. He had that same look of complete bafflement Hally'd seen on the faces of all those unimaginative adults, trying, without success, to fathom the possible merits a cute and cuddly toy such as this Elmo might possess.

Roger walked Hally to her car.

"Hally, I was wondering if you'd like to join me for dinner tomorrow? We could go to a movie. There's an Ingmar Bergman film playing downtown. Or we could—"

"I'm sorry, Roger. I'm, uh, busy tomorrow night," said Hally quickly.

The Gourmet Cupid

Roger looked nonplussed. "Another time, then?" he pulled his Armani scarf closer about his neck. "I know how busy you are. I'm pretty swamped myself, these days—what with the promotion and all." He sighed, but more with enthusiasm than weariness. "And as you said: 'Duty calls.'" He smiled, opening her door.

"Yes." Hally climbed into her car.

"I'll call you next month!" said Roger as she shut the door and started the engine.

"I'm busy next month," she muttered when she was veering toward Highway 94 and out of earshot.

But this was a lie.

"Okay, okay," she said to herself, "I know what you're thinking, but I didn't turn Roger down because of Ben Atkinson."

She sped through an amber light.

"And it's not as if I'm in love with him, or anything," she went on. "I mean, how could I fall in love with someone in that short a time? And with someone I barely know? It's totally unlike me! It's ridiculous! It's irrational, and it's—it's—"

She ran a red light just before the highway turnoff, and several cars honked furiously at her. She missed the entrance ramp, and cursed aloud.

She slowed down, and made her way into a web of back streets, halting suddenly behind a truck at the traffic lights. She tugged at her earlobe.

And it's true, she thought with a long surrendering sigh.

Hally removed the chunks of beef from the marinade (thank goodness Bel Abner made its own Burgundy Marinade product), and strained the vegetables. She glanced at her notes again. This was stage two of the beef bourguignon. The butter simmered in the pan, waiting to brown the beef. The timer showed four minutes. She was making good time.

The ring of the phone made her jump.

"Hello?"

"Hi. It's Ben."

Hally's heart stopped.

"Hally?"

"Yes, I'm here," Hally managed. Her hands had turned ice cold. "You, uh, just caught me in the middle of something."

"Oh, you have company?" The voice suddenly sounded distant.

Hally glanced over at the Bel Abner Gourmet products lining the countertop. "Actually, I'm cooking."

There came a low chuckle from the other end. "I hope you took notes. I probably missed all Lou Jay's good stuff. I'm going to be stuck eating appetizers and eggs the rest of my days."

A beat. Hally listened to the sounds of his breathing, not daring to move.

"Hally, I'd like to see you." The tone of his voice was low, hushed, as if he were afraid someone was listening in on the line.

She consulted her watch; it was almost nine. "I-I'm a little busy right now—"

"Yeah, me too. How about tomorrow?"

She had to go shopping, prepare the vichyssoise, and get ready the presentation for the Bel Abner campaign. "I can't. I-I have a business meeting the day after tomorrow. It's important."

"Yes, I know," she heard him mumble.

"Excuse me?"

"Oh—nothing." He cleared his throat. "I really need to speak with you, Hally."

"Well, can't you tell me over the phone?" *You're engaged to Veronica Wilmott again—is that it?*

"I think it would be best if we met in person," he answered after a moment.

"Look, Ben. We barely know each other. Who you see and what you do with your personal life is really none of my business."

"Actually, it has more to do with you than you think," said Ben enigmatically.

Hally glanced down at the pan on the stove. Smoke ribboned up from the burned butter like an SOS signal. The smoke detector on the ceiling began to shriek shrilly.

"Oh, darn!" she exclaimed into the phone, shoving the smoking pan onto the back element.

"Shall I call the fire department?" Ben inquired mildly. Hally detected the note of amusement in his voice.

"Ben, what do you want?" she said impatiently.

"Meet me tomorrow at the Arbre at one o'clock and I'll explain everything."

"I can't—"

"And bring your open mind."

"But I—"

"And my tuxedo jacket," he added before hanging up.

His tuxedo jacket. Funny how it had slipped her mind. That black thing hanging in her closet; it had befriended her other jackets, blended in nicely with the group. Hally had almost forgotten that it didn't belong there.

The smoke detector abated its piercing alarm as the oven fan blew the smoke out the side window. Hally shivered in the cold air, and gazed at the burned bottom of the pan, her cooking enthusiasm suddenly quashed. For the past two weeks she'd spent more hours in the kitchen than she had in the past two years.

After a moment, she closed the window and tramped over to the closet.

There it was, hanging between her leather coat and ski

jacket. Gingerly, she touched the sleeve, then brought it to her face. It still smelled like him, but mingling with his scent was her own familiar odor. Somehow, it seemed to her Ben's jacket belonged there, and Hally felt a strange reluctance to part with it.

What was it Ben needed to tell her? She didn't need to know that he and Veronica Wilmott were seeing each other—that much she'd guessed on her own. No, she didn't want to hear what he had to say; the worst thing he could do would be to apologize for leading her on— kissing her, when all that time he was seeing another woman. Veronica Wilmott: a beautiful, successful television actress (albeit, a ''B'' actress starring in ''B'' television dramas). How could Hally compete with that?

Hally resolved in that moment to cancel their lunch date. She remembered he was staying at the Kingsdale Hotel. In her mind she planned her escape. Escape? Yes, the less she saw of Ben Atkinson, the easier it would be to rid him from her system, Hally convinced herself.

''You going to lunch, Hally?'' asked Marla, fastening her coat. She gazed out at the snow-carpeted parking lot. ''Brrr . . . One more day of this and then I'm off to sun myself in my new bikini. In less than forty-eight hours I'll be sipping piña coladas on a warm sunny beach.'' She sighed.

''Don't rub it in,'' grumbled Danny, rising from his chair. ''Hally? You joining us? Marla's buying today.''

Marla narrowed her eyes at him, but her happy grin did not fade. ''You're taking advantage of my good mood.''

Hally patted her briefcase. ''I brought my lunch with me today,'' she said, glancing up at the clock: 12:25.

As soon as they left, Hally found the number for the Kingsdale Hotel in her Rolodex. She took several deep breaths, allowing a wave of calm to settle over her before she dialed.

"Kingsdale Hotel reception. How may I help you?" a man's voice answered.

"Hello. Yes, I'm, uh,—Ben Atkinson's room, please." Her heart pounded in her throat.

"Just a moment, please."

An orchestral version of "Someone Who Needs Me" chimed in her ear. It was abruptly interrupted by the receptionist's voice.

"I'm sorry, ma'am. We have no record of a Ben Atkinson staying here."

Hally was taken aback. "Are you sure?"

"Our computer guest list shows no Ben Atkinson," the voice repeated. "Are you certain you have the right name, ma'am? Or could it be that he is staying here with another guest?"

Veronica Wilmott? Hally almost uttered, but she only thanked the receptionist and hung up.

Darn! Her plan had hit a snag. She glanced over at the tuxedo jacket draped in the plastic laundry bag hanging next to her own coat. The sooner she got rid of it, the better, thought Hally. If she left now, she could still make it in time to meet Ben at the Arbre.

Hally kneaded her temples, considering this. Her other recourse was to call up the restaurant and leave a message. But there was still the matter of his tuxedo jacket.

Hally let the minutes click by. At five minutes after one, she called up the Arbre.

"The Arbre. Please hold."

In the background, Hally heard the sounds of clinking glasses and dishes, and the remote murmur of conversation: "... Lou Jay wants the big floral arrangements on the back tables ... I don't know, some big advertising convention, or something ... no, he's bringing in more chicken stock from one of his classes ..."

Lou Jay. So it was true! All their hard work went right back into his restaurant. Why, that wily old coot, thought Hally with a wan smile. Gourmet Hearts, indeed; Gourmet Slaves was more like it.

"Hello?" a new voice jarred her from her thoughts.

"Oh, hello. I'd like to leave a message for one of your customers. Ben Atkinson? He should be just coming in—or he might already be there. I don't know."

"Hmm . . . yes?" the voice waited.

"Uh, could you tell him, uh, Hally Chrisswell couldn't make it. Something, uh, came up."

"Ben Atkinson? I'm sorry—"

The name obviously didn't ring a bell. But Hally had assumed Ben was a regular at the Arbre, if not recognized in association with Veronica Wilmott.

"Maybe you could describe him for me?" prompted the host.

Hally conjured up an image of her cooking partner. "He's . . . about six-one, brown hair, green eyes—deep, penetrating eyes. Uh, he has a strong jawline, and he has full lips—" *Sensual, kissable lips,* she added silently, shutting her eyes.

"That's fine," the host interrupted her. "Can you hold on for a minute?"

"No, if you can just relay the messa—" But the host had already left, and the sounds of the restaurant filled her ears.

Hally waited, her heart bounding about her chest like an excited child. For a split second, she thought about hanging up. She knew that if she spoke with Ben, he'd manage to convince her to meet him. However, just as she was about to ring off, the voice of the host buzzed in her ear:

"I'm sorry, your party hasn't arrived yet. However, I'll relay the message as soon as he comes in."

Hally stared at the phone perched in its cradle. When

had she become such a coward? Where was the old Hally Chrisswell? The one with bravado and self-assurance, the one who exuded confidence and poise? She'd not managed to climb the rungs of her career acting like a timid, indecisive mouse. She was AE of a major campaign; there was no room now for a dip in her self-esteem.

She sighed, forcing herself upright, tilting up her chin. *Hally Chrisswell, don't forget who you are.*

However, as she cast a gaze in the direction of her boots—boots which Ben Atkinson had bought her—and rested her eyes on the tuxedo jacket, her shoulders slumped forward. Her stomach rumbled uneasily, and her pulse quickened.

What was it about that man? It was as though Ben Atkinson was in her blood, coursing through her veins, squeezing the muscles of her heart.

"I've got a virus," she grumbled aloud. "The Ben Atkinson virus."

Hally gritted her teeth and turned to her computer, and threw herself into her work. She'd just sweat it out of her system. What was it they say? Feed a cold; starve a fever? Or was it the other way around? She couldn't decide which.

Chapter Nine

As Hally sifted through her mail, her attention was suddenly caught by a small square envelope. The names on the return address read: Charles Radcliffe and Monique Weller.

Inside she found a wedding invitation. The entire front of it was decorated with a giant heart, and filling it were cartoonlike depictions of herbs and spices, with steaming pots and frying pans undoubtedly cooking up some delectable romantic gourmet meal. Folded inside were directions to the Lutheran church, along with a brief note penned by Monique:

> Fellow Gourmet Heart,
> We look forward to sharing our special day with you and Ben. Guess who's cooking dinner? Ha-ha! Don't worry, it's not us. Lou Jay promised us a magnificent romantic feast!

It was signed by both Monique and Charles.

Hally stared at the invitation. Monique had written, ''you and Ben''—taking for granted that they were a couple. But how had they managed to contact him? she wondered. She'd tried the Kingsdale Hotel again before she'd left work, but they still had no record of him staying there.

She hung Ben's tuxedo back in the closet. The jacket had become a link between them, a yet-to-be severed bond that kept alive in her the memory of that first kiss out on the patio, the silver-haired man playing the piano, singing.

And Hally found herself humming that same tune as she spread out on the dining-room table the agency mockups and concept sketches for the Bel Abner campaign.

Her afternoon meeting with Serina Heineault and Lyle Cramden had been brief but encouraging. The partners of Necessitas had approved her strategy proposals, but Serina appeared to be more impressed by the menu.

"I have a really good feeling about this, Hally," she told her. "Benton Abner paid us a visit this morning. It seems a representative from Prentice & Dreyer tried to contact his parents in Venice." She smirked. "Needless to say, Deliah Abner was less than pleased at having their privacy invaded."

"Benton Abner was here?"

Serina's dark red lips curved into a grim smile. "I know you're the AE on this project, but unfortunately, Benton had a pressing lunch engagement. But don't worry, I told him we had our best woman working on the campaign." Her thin brows drew together musingly. "Funny, he seemed more interested in you, Hally, than our campaign policies. If I didn't know better, I would've thought maybe he already knew you." Her dark eyes were fixed on Hally, and she inclined her head. "Unless . . . you *do* know Benton Abner."

"Uh, no. I've never met him," answered Hally, vaguely confused by Serina and Lyle Cramden's looks.

"Well, in any case, my 'spies,' " and Serina uttered this word with a conspiratorial grin, "tell me Prentice & Dreyer has rented a hall in the Kingsdale Hotel. They're serving some gourmet dishes, naturally—as is Westfall Enterprises, who I've just found out have reserved a private room at a restaurant called the Arbre."

"The Arbre?" echoed Hally.

"Apparently, the head chef there is a wiz at gourmet cooking," said Lyle Cramden, exchanging a concerned glance with Serina.

"Lou Jay," muttered Hally aloud.

"Oh? You've heard of this man?" Serina regarded Hally, her expression changing to bemusement.

Hally's chest suddenly tightened with doubt and panic. After the Abners tasted Lou Jay's cuisine, Hally's poached trout and beef bourguignon would seem like secondhand pig slop. Oh, no, she was doomed.

"Not to worry, Hally," assured Serina. "An intimate setting might be exactly what they're looking for. And your strategies and layouts are very impressive."

But you haven't tasted my cooking, thought Hally dismally.

Hally gazed about her newly decorated apartment. Tina had done a wonderful job, and in the evening light, the pale terra-cotta walls took on a soft romantic glow. On the table was a box in which Tina had packed a lace tablecloth, silver cutlery, and two brass candlesticks. The kitchen stood, strong and stalwart and proud, prepared for Hally's gourmet battle.

She sighed and groaned, her confidence crawling up into her appetizer escargot vol-au-vents, hiding in the cold depths of her vichyssoise soup, not daring to contemplate the poached trout or the evening's starring attraction: beef bourguignon. Only the hazelnut and roasted almond mousse cake sat ready, sealed in cellophane on the top rung of her refrigerator. Thankfully, the spongy foundation—the *genoise*, as Lou Jay had taught them—had turned out more or less even, if not sloping imperceptibly a little to one side. But her second attempt at the meringue had helped to conceal the flaw, and she was able to use Bel Abner Gourmet Filbert Paste as an alternative shortcut to attempting to create the hazelnut mousse spread herself.

Either the evening will be a disaster, she thought, *or a reenactment of a Three Stooges film.* Hally had a mental image of Randall and Deliah Abner excusing themselves after the meal, and running to the corner store to wolf down a bottle of Pepto-Bismol.

As she started toward her bedroom, she glimpsed the flashing red light on the answering machine. She reached over and played the message.

"I'm sure there's a good reason for you standing me up. But I really need to talk to you before tomorrow night. I—" Ben paused, and Veronica Wilmott's lilting voice rang out: "Be-e-en! They're waiting for us, honeybear." A dial tone sounded.

The second message, timed twenty minutes later, crackled with a spurt of static. Hally turned down the volume. A car phone, she guessed.

"Hello, Miss Chrisswell. This is Veronica Wilmott." There was a faint giggle, a coy, covetous sound that raised the shackles on the back of Hally's neck. "I'm calling to let you know Ben will be ... shall we say—*indisposed* all evening. As for this garment honeybear loaned you, you can drop it off at the Kingsdale Hotel where we're staying. *Ciao!*"

Hally's heart thudded and dropped like a stone in her stomach.

"A friend of the family, eh?" she muttered angrily, glowering at the machine. She shut it off with a bang of her wrist.

The phone rang. Hally gazed at it, and passed a hand over her French braid, untying it. She reached for the phone, then hesitated, deciding against answering it. Tonight she needed to concentrate on her vichyssoise and beef bourguignon, and thus far her mind was nowhere in the vicinity of the kitchen. She picked up Charles and

Monique's invitation, rubbing her thumb over the cartoonish heart as if to gather some inspiration from it.

The ringing of the phone finally stopped, and Hally glanced over at the concept sketches on the table. Marla had gone ahead and transcribed Hally's initial idea, a moment of weakness following her second class with Lou Jay in which she'd complained to Marla how the chef kept referring to the class as Gourmet Hearts and what a great concept it would make. But admittedly, it was a wonderfully original concept for the campaign, and Marla and Danny were immediately sold on the idea.

Well, it sold me. Hally sighed. She frowned at the cupid in the painting, feeling a sudden throbbing pain in her chest. She could hear again Veronica Wilmott's giggle and her singsong voice on the answering machine: "... where *we're* staying." *Together, no doubt,* Hally added with a silent leer.

She felt foolish and angry—angry at herself for being taken in by Ben Atkinson, a con man who had sold her heart a bill of tainted romance.

Now, all she wanted was a refund.

Hally regarded the two bottles of wine in her hands. "Would it be inappropriate to serve red *and* white, I wonder?"

Tina considered her dilemma. "Hmm . . . white goes with fish, but with beef bourguignon you've got to go with the red. Maybe—"

"I'd go with the rosé," suggested a voice behind them. "But that's only my opinion."

They turned around to gaze at the tall, bespectacled man with the thinning hair. He grinned at Hally.

"Charles! Hi!" exclaimed Hally. She introduced Tina, and her fellow Gourmet Heart grasped Tina's hand jovially. His face flushed, not from shyness, but from an inner confidence and exuberance that made the blue eyes behind the thick lenses light up.

"I received your wedding invitation yesterday," Hally told him.

Charles laughed. "We invited the whole cooking class—even that journalist, Karl MacAvoy. The design on the invitations was Monique's idea. She thought everyone would get a kick out of it."

"It was, uh, very original," said Hally. She replaced the wine on the rack. "Uh, I should tell you that Ben and—"

"Oh, I just spoke with him a couple of minutes ago. He was going out as I was coming in," said Charles. "Lucky coincidence, really. Lou Jay only had his old address in Chicago, and the hotel—" Charles waved his hand. "Well, that doesn't matter anymore—now that he's living in Milwaukee. And of course, we just figured you'd tell him."

Hally anxiously gazed behind her to the liquor store entrance. "Ben was here?"

Charles gazed at her, furrowing his brow. "Ben was just—"

Hally winced and shuffled her feet uncomfortably. "Actually, Charles, Ben and I—"

"Did I tell you I asked him to be my best man?" Charles grinned.

"Y-your best man?" Hally's eyes widened.

"Yes. Seems my brother won't be back from the Solomon Islands in time for the wedding." Charles sighed. "But that's what you get for springing into something like this. You know, I don't think I'd ever done one spontaneous, impulsive act in my whole life until I enrolled in Lou Jay's class."

Hally could believe it. She and Charles, she guessed, were very similar: cautious, organized, responsible. "Uh, about Ben. He and I—"

"There's Monique!" Charles made a frantic gesture at the window, but Monique did not notice, and kept walking. Charles turned to Hally and squeezed her arm. "I better hustle. I promised my bride-to-be I'd help with the floral arrangements. I'm glad I bumped into you, Hally. Monique and I were beginning to think you and Ben had broken up." He waved to Tina. "Nice to have met you!" he called, hurrying out the exit.

Tina gazed at Hally, eyebrows raised inquiringly. "What was that all about?"

Hally swept another anxious glance about the liquor store, but Ben was nowhere in sight. Relief settled over her, but her heart was clamoring in her chest. She shrugged off her friend's curious look and proceeded down the adjacent row of wines.

"Your friend, he thinks you and Ben are seeing each other," said Tina.

Hally selected a bottle of rosé, and inspected the label at length.

"You have it bad for him, don't you?"

"Who?"

"Who? Ben Atkinson, who."

Hally glanced up at her friend, hoping her exasperation concealed what she was really feeling.

But Tina only shook her head. "It's written all over your face, Hal."

"I'll get over it," mumbled Hally.

This time is was Tina's turn to be exasperated. "You heard your friend. Ben Atkinson is living here now. In Milwaukee. Why don't you just call him up—"

"Tina, it's hopeless. Trust me." She recalled the real estate business card in the pocket of his tuxedo. Was this what Ben and Veronica had been planning all along? To buy a home here, settle down, raise a family? Hally imagined the two of them cozying together before a roaring fireplace, toasting their future in Milwaukee. But why

Milwaukee? Hadn't Hally read somewhere that Veronica Wilmott lived in Los Angeles?

"I just want to get through this dinner, Tina." She grimaced, grasping the bottle of rosé by the neck.

Tina didn't respond, but her disapproving silence said more than enough.

Hally went over her list for the umpteenth time, and consulted her watch again. The beef bourguignon had been cooking for close to two hours, and the snails sat warming beside it, packed snugly in their pastry vol-au-vents. On the stove the escargot sauce simmered, the steamer ready for the broccoli and snow peas, while the hand-cut potato *frites* lay on the cutting board awaiting their frying fate.

Hally opened the refrigerator, and cast another look at her chilled vichyssoise, eyeing the hazelnut and roasted almond mousse cake which seemed suspiciously flatter than a moment ago. She assured herself the cake was fine, that it wasn't shrinking. She pulled out the four trout fillets.

Thank goodness she'd had the foresight to buy an extra fillet, for earlier this morning Hally'd received an urgent call on her machine from Serina who informed her that Randall and Deliah Abner's eldest son, Benton Abner, was also coming to dinner. The news had given Hally a little nervous jolt, but what was one more guest? she told herself.

So what if the gossip about Benton Abner was true? So what if he was a flirt, and as charming and handsome as he was purported to be? Gossip, in her experience, was always a vehicle for exaggeration and fantasy. Besides, Hally had never been one to be intimidated by simple good looks and charm. And she could handle a little flirtation.

Ben Atkinson suddenly zoomed into her thoughts, and

Hally forced him out of her mind with a frustrated sigh. There was always an exception to the rule.

She peered in the window of the microwave at her vinaigrette. She glanced at her watch; they'd be here any minute. Her heart gave a quick panicky lurch, and her stomach muscles contracted.

"Calm yourself, Hally. You've done this a hundred times before—well, not this, exactly." She gazed at the pots on the stove doubtfully. "You're a Gourmet Heart, Hally. You can do this," she urged, squaring her shoulders and tilting up her chin. Her fingers passed over her tight, neat French braid, and she smoothed the nonexistent wrinkles in her suit skirt. Maybe she didn't look like a gourmet cook, but she felt positively drenched with the spicy aroma of it.

The doorbell rang, and she jumped, her blood freezing in its venal path. Hally wrung her hands trying to restart her circulatory system, and took several deep breaths. She reached down and rearranged a fork, adjusted the napkins. The candles! Should she light the candles now, or later? She ran into the kitchen opening drawers. Where were the stupid matches?

The doorbell rang again, and Hally heard a low murmur of laughter. She strode toward the door, pausing before the hall mirror to check herself. The amber eyes that stared back at her were wide, the pupils slightly dilated. Her cheeks were flushed, her skin glowing. A thin blond tendril escaped from her hairline, and Hally swiftly tucked it back inside the braid.

She opened the door, coming face-to-face with a tall woman with an aristocratic face. She was wearing a brown suede coat lined with faux leopard fur, and her leather-gloved hands were clasped in front of her. The eyes, a luminous hazel green, crinkled in a greeting smile, and her small but full lips curved upward, showing even white teeth. Hally recalled the press photos, and thought Deliah Abner looked much more impressive in person. And she found herself taking an instant liking to the woman.

"Hello, Miss Chrisswell. I'm Deliah Abner. We were afraid we almost had the wrong apartment," she said, the deep pleasantness of her voice filling the hallway.

"Please, won't you come in?" Hally smiled, feeling the tension sliding away from her shoulders.

Randall Abner rubbed his gloved hands together. "Ah! Warmth! Why we left Venice to come back to this—" He sniffed. "What is that incredible smell?"

Hally grinned. Here was an altogether different person from the austere-featured man she'd expected from the photographs. In fact, he reminded her a little of her own father. And her father had a giant appetite.

This wasn't going to be so bad after all, she thought, taking Deliah Abner's coat.

"Oh, and what a charming apartment!" She glanced over at her husband. "Reminds me a little of that place we had in Paris, remember, Randall?"

"How could I forget? Benton was a two-year-old terror—Benton?" He glanced behind him. "Now where did that boy get off to?"

"I'm right here, Dad."

Hally dropped Deliah Abner's coat. A vise seemed to squeeze her ribcage together as she stared breathlessly at the man standing in the doorway.

"Oops. Let me get that," said the man, bending down.

"This is our son, Benton Abner," Deliah introduced proudly.

"Ben—Benton Abner?" Hally's throat managed to squeak out, as she gazed, mesmerized, into the familiar face. *What are you doing here?* she wanted to scream. *Your name isn't Benton Abner—it's Ben Atkinson!*

"How do you do, Miss Chrisswell." He slid his hand

into her palm, and squeezed her fingers, his eyes regarding her steadily, silently relaying a message.

Randall shifted his gaze between them. He frowned. "Do you two know each other?"

The eddying in Hally's head suddenly stopped. Her senses sharpened, and she could feel a slow anger prickling beneath her skin. Her smile was thin. "Apparently not," she replied coolly.

Deliah and Randall glanced curiously at their host, then over to Ben.

"Am I missing something? Benton?" Randall Abner inclined his head toward his son.

Ben and Hally exchanged looks, Ben smiling ruefully while Hally's amber eyes flashed dangerously beneath her polite veneer.

Neither of them spoke for a moment.

"Well," said Deliah Abner, finally. "I smell garlic. A wonderful aroma, garlic. It stirs the appetite."

"It's supposed to be an aphrodisiac," added Ben, helping Hally put away the coats. "Let me guess." He spied his tuxedo jacket in the laundry bag, and was distracted for a moment, losing his train of thought. "Er, a shrimp dish, right?"

"Escargots," Hally corrected him, dodging his gaze. She smiled at his parents. "Won't you come in and sit down?"

"Escargots? You mean, snails? When did we—?" Ben cut himself off. He adjusted his tie and combed his fingers through his hair.

Hally thought he looked strangely out of place in his dark pinstripe suit. For some reason she could only picture him in jeans and that leather bomber jacket—and a tuxedo, of course. But the suit lent him a stiff business air, a false armor that did not mesh well with his devil-may-care personality.

What am I doing? thought Hally. *I didn't even know*

his real name, so what makes me think I know anything about his real personality?

"Escargots. Hah!" Randall slapped Benton on the back. "Remember that time Veronica cooked us that dinner in L.A.? Goodness, what a disaster! I remember I lost a filling that night biting into a piece of garlic bread."

"Veronica? Veronica Wilmott?" uttered Hally without thinking.

"Yes. You know of her, then?" said Deliah, not looking overly surprised. "I don't watch too much television, but I'm told Veronica has good film presence—whatever that means. The way they talk about her, you'd think Veronica was an angel. My, my. She was far from an angel when she was a young girl, I'll tell you." Deliah clucked, shaking her head. "Even then she always had her eye on Benton—"

"Mom," Ben interrupted her, shooting her a warning, pleading look.

"Can't seem to get rid of her," said Randall Abner gruffly. "Sticks to Benton like a fly to flypaper." He grinned. "But it seems my son enjoys bachelorhood too much. We're just hoping that one day the right girl will come along and sweep him off his feet."

Ben caught Hally's eye, and he winked. She fought down a blush. What nerve!

"It's not that we don't like Veronica." Deliah wiped a piece of lint off Ben's shoulder. "Benton and Veronica were once engaged, in fact."

"Mmm . . . these escargots smell delicious," said Ben, a little too loudly. He steered his father into the dining room.

"I admire what you're doing, Miss Chrisswell," said Deliah Abner.

Hally looked at Ben's mother, panic rising to her

throat. Was she really that transparent? "I—uh, well, it's a long story—"

"It's been a while since I spent an evening in the kitchen preparing a meal. And you're doing this all by yourself." Deliah Abner surveyed the table with a delighted smile. "Necessitas must put a lot of faith in you."

"I—thank you, Mrs. Abner. I enjoy cooking," she fibbed, although, she thought, was it a lie? In retrospect, she couldn't say she'd exactly detested all the shopping and decorating, and she had to admit she'd rather enjoyed planning and preparing this meal.

"I especially like to cook for those I know will appreciate it," she added.

"The Abners do enjoy a good meal." Deliah smiled. She leaned closer to Hally, whispering confidentially. "But word to the wise, dear. Mixing business with pleasure doesn't go well with Randall. Like me, my husband likes to savor his food. As for Benton, well—he's quite new to all this." She winked at Hally. It was Ben's wink, Hally noticed.

Hally digested this information, and wondered at the long look Deliah Randall gave her. Had she guessed that she and Ben did, in fact, know each other? Were Ben's parents privy to his deceit? She wondered how much he'd told them.

But Hally was over her momentary shock, and she could feel herself changing gears, her practised business acuity moving to the forefront of her thoughts. Her nervousness waned, and she adjusted her focus. She knew what she needed to do: she was going to get through this evening alive, and she was going to try her darnedest to land this account.

Ben stared at her from the door of the kitchen. "Can I help, Hally?"

The Gourmet Cupid 161

And she was going to land this account *without* his help, she told herself firmly.

"That's very kind of you, Mr. Abner," she replied slowly, "but I think I can handle this on my own, thank you."

"Please, call me Ben." His green eyes searched hers.

"Not Benton?" offered Hally, her sarcasm as subtle as running him over with a snow plow.

"Ben. I like Ben."

"You haven't been called Ben since you were four years old." Randall Abner chuckled. He unbuttoned his jacket and sat down. "And that was Grammy Belena. She thought 'Benton' sounded too much like a car."

"Your middle name wouldn't happen to be . . . Atkinson, would it?" Hally addressed Ben, her voice chilly.

Ben shot her a sheepish grin which his parents did not catch.

"Benton Harlan Abner," said Deliah, sitting next to her husband. "My, when you say it aloud like that, he *does* sound a little like an automobile."

Well, your son did manage to run me over, said Hally silently.

"So what's your middle name, Hally?" asked Ben, his eyes challenging her.

Hally hesitated. She lifted her chin slightly. "Christina."

"Oh, what a pretty name: Hally Christina Chrisswell."

"My mother named me after her favorite poet: Christina Rossetti."

A bright smile broke across Deliah Abner's aristocratic face. "Why, she's one of my favorite poets, as well!"

Ben gave Hally a thumbs-up, and winked behind his mother's back. Hally felt her cheeks grow warm. So far, so good, she thought as she opened the oven door to pull out the appetizers.

Ben rose to help her clear the first-course dishes.

"Please, sit. I can do this." She smiled at him tepidly.

His green eyes searched hers, almost imploringly. "I'd like to help, Hally."

"Part of being a good cook is cleaning up after yourself," she said.

"Being a good cook also involves being able to delegate duties," countered Ben.

Hally thought about Lou Jay and the way he had organized his kitchen, delegating his class—his Gourmet Hearts.

"You know"—Deliah Abner pressed her napkin to her lips and folded it on the table—"Benton has a point." She stood up.

Randall Abner glanced at his wife, and noting her determined expression, he sighed. "The world is changing," he muttered, and pushed his chair back.

"No, no. Please, sit. Digest your food. I can handle this," protested Hally.

"Yes, she can handle everything," murmured Ben. "Mom, Dad, you can help with the dishes. Hally and I will take it from here."

Hally gazed at Ben helplessly as he sidled past her into the kitchen with the dirty dishes.

"Am I ingratiating myself enough?" he said when they were out of earshot of his parents.

"Just put them on the counter."

"I think my parents like you."

"Great. Now, go sit down."

"Your story about that chef, Louis Diat, was priceless. How he had to endure all those morons who kept complaining about the vichyssoise being cold—"

"Ben—or rather, *Benton*. I think I can take it from

here," she said, tossing the potato *frites* into the boiling oil. They crackled loudly. "I'll just be a few minutes."

"I'm sorry I didn't tell you who I was. But you have to understand—"

"I understand."

"No, you don't."

Hally lapsed into silence. No, she didn't understand. But what did it matter now? She opened the oven door and peeked in on her beef bourguignon. Was it overcooked? Her timing was a little off, and Ben's presence in the kitchen was making her nervous.

"So, how come you stood me up?"

"I—I had to work."

"You could have called me."

"I did. The Kingsdale Hotel had no record of you," said Hally, watching the *frites* caramelize in the oil. "Now I know why."

"Look, can we get a coffee later? You owe me that much."

"I owe you—?!"

"Everything all right in here?" Deliah Abner stood in the doorway. "Can you use another pair of hands? By the way, Hally, that sauce you used for the trout was exquisite. What is your secret?"

Hally flushed. "Actually, uh, I used a Bel Abner product—Dijon Vinaigrette."

Deliah smiled. "Yes, I know. Randall invented that recipe—back in the old days when he used to cook." She laughed. "Yes, believe it or not, there was a time when you couldn't get Randall *out* of the kitchen." She glanced at her son. "Well, I'll leave you two to get on with whatever you're doing."

"Your mother's nice," said Hally, after Deliah left.

"She knows how to read people."

Hally eyed him sharply. "You didn't tell her about—"

"No. But I think she suspects we already know each other. They didn't even know I was taking that gourmet class. I wanted it to be a surprise, and then I had to fly to Venice—" He paused, chewing on his lip. "Hally, I have a confession to make—"

"Excuse me." Hally scooped out the *frites* onto the paper towel and dabbed the excess oil.

" 'The secret of the perfect *frite*,' " quoted Ben, " 'lies in the oil temperature.' " His green eyes gazed at her challengingly. " 'Fry them twice—' "

Hally tossed them back into the oil. She could hear Lou Jay ululating the words with his large hands gesticulating passionately. " 'Fry them fast,' " she cut in, her amber eyes meeting Ben's briefly. She picked up a spoon and stirred. " 'Also movement is important.' "

" 'So that the oil may crisp the outside of the *frite*,' " injected Ben, stepping closer to her, " 'but always leaving the inside tender—vulnerable.' "

Hally tugged on her earlobe, trying to concentrate. She could smell his musky new-spring suede scent mingling with the aroma of the beef bourguignon. Her eye went to the painting on the wall, the cupid seeming now more smug than ever. She realized, at that moment, she wanted Ben to kiss her—embrace her as he had that afternoon in this very apartment, after he'd carried her up two flights of stairs.

Hally pointed vaguely toward the stove. "You can, uh, take out the beef bourguignon, if you want."

"Only if you agree to meet me for coffee later."

"Fine." Hally pursed her lips. "I can do it myself."

Ben drew himself rigid and moved away from her. "Yes, you can handle everything, all by yourself. You don't need anyone, do you?" he said coldly.

Hally bit back a retort. *I need you, Ben,* a voice answered inside her head.

"Okay," she said, straining the cooked *frites* from the oil.

Ben paused at the doorway. "Okay, what?"

"I'll meet you for coffee later," she said, not looking at him. "To hear your confession."

"Thank you, my sweet and beautiful priest." He grinned, reaching in the oven for the beef bourguignon. "My Gourmet Heart," he added, his murmur barely audible.

Hally fumbled with the *frites*, nearly upsetting the basket. "Gourmet Heart": that she had never heard these words. But her entire campaign was contingent on this concept. Would the Abners go for it?

"Ready?" Ben watched her curiously.

Hally smiled and nodded. Her Gourmet Heart fluttered, having digested the escargots, the vichyssoise, and the trout. Now it made room for her crisp *frites*, the beef bourguignon, and her hazelnut and roasted almond mousse cake. However, she judged there still might yet be enough room left in her Gourmet Heart for Ben.

Hally gazed at her reflection critically. She'd washed her face and changed into jeans and a long-sleeved blouse. After a moment's thought, she loosened her hair from her French braid, and let the crinkly tresses fall across her shoulders. No longer did she look the part of the advertising executive. No, she was Hally Chrisswell, a woman setting aside her career for one evening. Tonight, she would show her "vulnerable" side.

The phone rang. Hally picked it up.

"Hi. How'd it go?" said Tina.

"Not bad, I guess—except for one huge surprise you are *not* going to believe."

"Oooh. Give me all the details."

Hally glanced at her watch. "I can't now. I'm already

ten minutes late." She hung up and grabbed her purse off the table and hurried out of the apartment.

As she sped down 124th Street toward the Arbre, she suddenly remembered Ben's tuxedo jacket. Oh, but it was too late to turn back. Darn that jacket! Would she ever be rid of it?

But the thought of her being with Ben tonight—alone, sharing an intimate conversation, their bodies close with eyes locked onto each other—made her suddenly glad she'd left his jacket at home. It was, she admitted, an excuse to see him again.

She had to park the car in the lot behind the Arbre, the place was so crowded. Hally wished suddenly she'd dressed more appropriately as she strode past a black limousine and an exiting group of people wearing fur hats and fur-collared coats. The wind stung her cheeks and blew Hally's hair across her eyes.

"Yes, Miss?"

Hally frantically ran her fingers through her long blond tresses. "Uh, hi. I'm Hally Chrisswell. I'm here to meet Ben Atkin—Ben Abner," she amended, smiling at the maître d'.

He glanced down at her Canadian leather boots, his expression uncertain.

"I'm, uh, I'm afraid I'm not exactly dressed for this place," she confessed uneasily.

The maître d' shrugged, offering her a small smile. "A guest of Ben Abner's is a guest of the Arbre's, Miss Chrisswell. Please, follow me."

He led her through the restaurant, and Hally tugged on her ear self-consciously, avoiding the looks of the other patrons. They strode past an archway partition made of wide mahogany beams, and Hally saw two people holding hands across the table: Veronica Wilmott—and Ben.

Ben rose as she approached.

"May I take your coat, Miss Chrisswell?" offered the maître d'.

Hally was attempting to rein in her anger, but she was already seeing red. What a fool she was! She'd not wanted to acknowledge it, but a small part of her had hoped Ben would tell her that all her assumptions about him and Veronica Wilmott were unfounded—that the two of them weren't romantically involved.

"Thank you, but I can't stay," she said tightly.

Ben looked at her, confused. "Veronica Wilmott, Hally Chrisswell," he introduced. "Hally, won't you sit down? What's the hurr—"

"Nice to meet you, Veronica." Hally accepted the well-manicured hand.

Veronica swept a cursory gaze over her jeans and blouse. Hally zipped up her jacket. "What a charming outfit," purred Veronica, fingering her pearls which dangled to the cleavage of her black, sequined dress. She took in Hally's Canadian boots with a faint smile. "Please, won't you join us? Benny was just telling me about the meal you cooked for Deliah and Randall. How nice to be so... domestic." She uttered this last word as if it were a dirty word.

"It was terrific," said Ben enthusiastically. "Hally, please sit—"

"I'm sorry. I really have to go."

"But you just got here," said Ben in bewilderment.

"Oh, what a shame. Timing is everything, isn't it? Ben's just agreed to accompany me back to L.A. tomorrow." Veronica tossed back her glistening chestnut hair. "These television directors can be so temperamental. No patience whatsoever."

"Yes, well—have a nice trip, Miss Wilmott, Mr. Atkinson. I'm sorry, but I really have to go," the iciness in her voice broke suddenly.

"Hally, wait—"

But Hally was already making her way back toward the entrance. The maître d' glanced up from his host lectern, and nodded at her.

"Hally!"

Hally gave the maître d' a quick smile, and started for the door. "Say hello to Lou Jay, will you?"

She ran around to the lot in the back, her heart pounding. She heard Ben calling her name, but she didn't stop. *Fool! Fool!* her head echoed. She climbed into her Mustang, and nosed out of the lot. In her rearview mirror, she saw Ben waving at her, his tie and jacket blowing in the wind.

"Good-bye, Ben Atkinson; good-bye, Benton Abner," she growled softly.

Good-bye, my Gourmet Heart, a voice deep inside her added.

Chapter Ten

Tina showed up at her door. "Why aren't you answering your phone? I've been calling you for three days!"

"I'm sick."

"Yeah?" Tina cocked an eyebrow, taking in Hally's disheveled hair, her rumpled bathrobe. "Hmm... You don't look sick."

Hally paused in her tracks and gave her friend a withering look.

"Granted, you don't look yourself," said Tina, closing the door behind her. "But I've seen you with the Hong Kong flu, remember, and you looked better then than you do now."

Hally plopped back down into the nest of blankets she'd made on the couch, and turned off the television.

"The apartment looks great," said Tina, admiring her handiwork.

"Okay, Mrs. Columbo. You finished?"

"Okay, so you didn't get the account—"

"Oh, we got it, all right," said Hally tonelessly.

"You did? Well, but—that's good, isn't it?" Tina sat down on the ottoman.

"Hmm... I don't know. I think there might've been some outside influence—or rather *inside* influence."

"Huh?" Tina frowned, not understanding.

"Remember that huge surprise I mentioned on the phone?"

Tina nodded, leaning forward. "You left me hanging for three days! So?"

"Well, guess who showed up for dinner on Thursday?"

"Who? I don't know—Colonel Mustard? Professor Plum?" Tina gazed at her friend impatiently.

"Ben Atkinson." Hally's mouth twisted as she uttered the name. "Or should I say, *Benton Abner.*"

"Benton Abner? You mean—"

"Ben Atkinson is Benton Harlan Abner."

Tina slapped her thigh. "I knew I recognized him from somewhere!" She laughed and scratched her head. "But why would he—?"

"He lied to me." Hally lay back across the couch, and stared up at the ceiling.

After a moment, Tina said, "I suppose he had a good enough reason. Maybe he thought it might influence you if you knew who he really was."

Hally grunted. That thought had already occurred to her. But he'd lied about other things, too—namely Veronica Wilmott.

"So, did he explain why he lied?" Tina plodded into the kitchen, noticed the phone lying off the hook, and replaced it. "No, I guess you didn't give him the chance."

"Oh, I gave him a chance," said Hally aloud to herself. She glanced toward the kitchen. "Don't hang up the phone—"

The phone rang.

"Don't answer it!"

Tina picked up the phone. "Just a sec," she said into the receiver. "It's for you!"

"I don't want to talk to him." grumbled Hally miserably. "Hang up."

"It's Monique Weller."

"Who? Oh." Hally slid reluctantly out from her cozy cave of blankets, and took the phone.

"Hi, Monique."

"Hally. Finally! I've been trying to reach you, but your phone's been busy all morning."

"Really? Huh. Must be some trouble with the line," lied Hally. Tina rolled her eyes, opened the refrigerator, and inspected the contents. She pulled out the half-eaten hazelnut and roasted almond mousse cake.

"Anyway," began Monique, "I know this is short notice, Hally, but I was wondering if you'd like to be my maid of honor at my wedding." And before Hally had a chance to respond Monique rattled on:

"Unfortunately my best friend, Darlene, can't make it. She's stuck somewhere in Denmark excavating Viking runes or something. So I need you to meet me this weekend at Generation Gown. You know where it is? It's by the Iron Block Building—"

"Yes, I know where it is," said Hally. She passed by that shop everyday when she went to lunch. "But, Monique. Not to say that I'm not honored you chose me to be your maid of honor—"

"Well, it works out perfectly, doesn't it? Seeing that Ben is Charles's best man, I mean," said Monique cheerfully.

Hally winced. She'd forgotten that little detail. Well, she'd better set the record straight, before—

"It's almost as if fate has smiled upon us. I'm telling you, Hally, Lou Jay's gourmet cooking class has changed my life. I'm not the same woman I used to be. It's like—like I've taken on a new identity."

"You're not the only one," muttered Hally. "Uh, listen, Monique, I'd love to be your maid of honor, but—"

"Wonderful! I'll see you Saturday, then? Two o'clock? I've decided to incorporate a green theme into the wedding, and I'd really like to know what you think. Did you know that they can grow green carnations? Oh! I'm so excited, Hally! I can't thank you enough!''

Hally listened to the dial tone for a few seconds, then hung up. After a moment's thought, she picked up the receiver and set it next to the phone's cradle.

"Another wedding?" inquired Tina.

"More complications." Hally groaned.

"You know, if you just call Ben—"

"He's in L.A.," said Hally. "With Veronica Wilmott."

"But I thought he said—"

"I don't take any stock in what Ben Atkinson—or rather, what *Benton Abner* says anymore."

Tina eyed the phone. "I bet he's trying to call you right now. You should at least give him a chance to explain—"

A recorded message interrupted her:

"Please hang up and try your call again; please hang up and try your call again..."

Tina reached for the phone, but Hally stopped her.

"No, I just want to forget about him."

Tina regarded her friend, a faint, wry smile turning up the corners of her mouth. "So you *do* think he's trying to call," she said. "What are you afraid of, Hal?"

I'm afraid he's not *going to call,* answered Hally silently.

A series of piercing beats shrilled from the receiver. "Ben... Ben... Ben..." it shrieked.

Hally grimaced and stuck her fingers in her ear.

"Congratulations on landing the Bel Abner account, Hally!" Serina shook Hally's hand. "I hope you're feeling better today."

Hally smiled and sat down. "Much better, thank you. Must have been a twenty-four-hour bug, or something. I feel like... my old self again." She passed her hand over her French braid, and straightened her suit jacket.

"Well, I have some news that will make you feel even better." Serina nodded to Lyle Cramden. "Randall and Deliah were very impressed by your campaign ideas, Hally—not to mention the gourmet meal you prepared. And Benton Abner faxed us from Los Angeles. He seems to think very highly of you."

Hally blushed, and struggled to regain her composure.

"Maybe you can invite the board over for one of your famous gourmet meals sometime." Lyle winked at her.

Hally swallowed back a wince.

"Speaking of which," said Serina, "the board has recommended that you officially be promoted to Advertising Executive, effective January of this coming year." Serina grinned. "Congratulations, Hally!"

Hally blinked and rose to her feet dazedly. She accepted Lyle Cramden's hand, and turned to receive Serina's bear hug.

"We know you'll do Necessitas proud," said Serina confidently.

As Hally turned to leave, Serina suddenly stopped her.

"Oh, Hally? Here." She handed her an envelope. "This came for you this morning."

Hally glanced at it. It was addressed to Necessitas, in care of Hally Christina Chrisswell. There was no return address. But the telltale postmark was clue enough: Beverly Hills, Los Angeles.

She stuck it into her briefcase, and returned to her office.

"Marla called from Jamaica," said Danny as she strode in. "She says congrats on the Bel Abner account. She wishes she could be here to celebrate."

"No she doesn't."

Danny laughed. "You're right, she doesn't. So what's the news from head office?"

"You're looking at the team's new AE."

"Wow! Hally, that's great!" He rose from his chair and gave her a hug.

"Hey!" He looked at her, frowning. "Am I actually more excited than you?"

Hally forced a smile onto her face. "I'm just letting it sink in right now."

Danny's concerned expression was peppered now with curiosity and interest. He observed her for a moment as she sat down at her desk, arranging objects about the perimeter.

"You know, Hally, you've been acting a little strange lately—different. You seem a little . . . distracted. Not to pry into your personal affairs or anything, but—"

"It's nothing, Danny. Just the holidays, I suppose," said Hally with a reassuring smile. "Nothing I can't handle."

The letter was burning a hole in her briefcase, nibbling at her thoughts like a gluttonous mouse. She'd wanted to tear it up, but she couldn't bring herself to do it.

Finally, as Hally slid in between the warm bedcovers, she reached down and fished it out of the briefcase. She turned it around in her hands, and tore it open.

Hally,
I had a cognac after a meal the other day and I saw your eyes. I look forward to seeing those eyes at the wedding.
Your Gourmet Heart, Ben

Hally lay back against the pillow, Ben's note still clutched in her hand. She closed her eyes, thinking back to the evening of the Bel Abner presentation.

After adjourning themselves into the living room, bellies full of beef Bourguignon and mousse cake, Randall

Abner had lit his cigarillo—after politely requesting permission from their hostess. And while Deliah Abner was swatting away the smoke with a disapproving glare at her husband, Hally had nervously occupied herself preparing the conceptual sketches and campaign mockups. Ben, standing next to her, was holding up a glass, gazing intently at the rich amber liquid.

"Now I recognize the color of those eyes," he had murmured, loud enough for Hally to hear. He had looked over at her, staring at her with a scrutinizing, but lazy, satisfied grin.

"Cognac eyes," he had murmured, his words caressing her cheeks.

Now, as Hally recalled the moment, she felt the rekindling of heat return to her face—

Nonsense! Cognac eyes. Gourmet Hearts. She gave a derisive snort. Romantic malarky. Hally glanced back at Ben's note, and was about to ball it up when she saw the postscript scribbled on the bottom.

(P.S.) Bring my tuxedo, will ya?

Hally made a frustrated gurgling noise in her throat and balled up the letter. She threw it at the wastepaper basket being used as a doorstop.

She missed.

Ah! If only the cupid could have been so inaccurate, she thought miserably.

Hally clutched tightly the bouquet of rosebuds and green carnations. The baby's breath drooped a little, threatening to fall out. Under her arms, beads of sweat gathered, and as she strode down the center aisle of the church, the heavy swish of taffeta crashed in her ears. She prayed the green material wouldn't give away her nervousness.

A few familiar faces loomed up from the pews: Karl MacAvoy snapped a photo, his minirecorder poised on the edge of his seat; Michael, with hair greased back, winked at her, and his long-legged cooking partner tightened her hold on his arm and smiled warily at Hally. Lou Jay beamed like a proud father, his bright blue polyester suit practically bursting at the seams. Hally grinned at the gourmet chef, feeling her anxiety beginning to melt away.

Despite the austere architecture of the church, the hallowed building glimmered and glowed with the bride and groom's happiness. Even the stern, hawklike minister caught himself pausing in his sermon to smile faintly up at the couple.

Hally listened, with head cocked to the side, until she suddenly became aware of the pair of eyes watching her. She swiveled her gaze left, and met Ben's stare. He swiftly returned his attention to Charles and Monique, who bowed their heads together, spectacles to spectacles, sealing their vows with a kiss. Hally inadvertently shivered, a thrilling chill rippling up through the soles of her feet.

When they all strode out of the church, Hally drew in a long, sighing breath.

"Who knew they could grow green carnations?" Ben fingered the bright green flower in his lapel.

Hally tugged on her earlobe, and barely achieved a polite, if not, civil smile.

"They make a great couple, don't they?" He gazed back at Charles and Monique who were shaking hands with the minister.

"Smile!" Karl MacAvoy aimed his 35-mm. camera at them.

Ben pulled Hally to him and kissed her. Her maid of honor bouquet flattened against his chest while a series of flashes haloed about them.

Hally pushed him away. "Why, you—"

Karl shoved his mini tape recorder in their faces, flashing them a greedy, toothy smile. "Do I hear more wedding bells in the near future, Ben—uh, Mr. Abner, Miss Chrisswell?"

Ben gazed at the mini–tape recorder. "Well . . . you could say we're in the process of cooking up a romance." He grinned.

Hally glared at him and flared her nostrils. "I think I smell something burning in the oven," she harrumphed.

Karl MacAvoy's eyes grew wide with excitement, and Hally suddenly realized how her statement might be construed by this journalist.

"You mean to say that there might be a wee one on the way—"

"What I mean to say is that Ben and I are just friends—oh, get that thing out of my face!" She swatted away the minirecorder and turned on her heel, threading her way back through the crowd.

You should learn to keep your mouth shut, Hally admonished silently. *And keep away from Ben; you'll be all right as long as you stay clear of that man,* she advised herself.

"Hally! Where're you going? We're doing photographs in a few minutes." Monique linked her arm in hers. "And I need my maid of honor. Have you met my parents?"

Hally donned her best composed face, and smiled mutely, preparing herself for the onslaught of formalities. The worst was over, she thought.

"Wasn't that nice of Charles and Monique to have us pose together?" said Ben. "Monique promised to send me the last one. You know, the one with us kissing. It will look perfect sitting on my new fireplace mantel."

"Yes, that is if you want to stoke the fire of a certain

television actress," retorted Hally, taking a gulp of her champagne.

Ben's brows drew together. "Who—? Oh, you mean ... ol' Veronica." He laughed. "Oh, you don't have to worry about that." His green eyes twinkled in amusement.

"I guess I'm just an old-fashioned girl," said Hally tartly.

She'd finally read the article in *Life Worth Living*. The photograph of Ben in the magazine didn't do him justice, she thought, stealing a glance at him over the rim of her fluted glass. The writer had dubbed him an "intellectual flirt," itemizing Benton Abner's likes and dislikes in a woman as if they were a grocery list—ingredients for making a romantic dinner. Hally was vaguely surprised to discover he enjoyed classical music and actually played the violin. There had been no mention of gourmet food—only that he admitted to being able to ice skate better than he could cook, and ice skating wasn't exactly his best sport, he'd joked to the interviewer.

"So you play the violin," said Hally, after a moment.

"You read the article. I'd hoped you'd have forgotten about it after I—" He grinned. "Okay, I was a little sneaky, I admit it."

Hally blinked. "It was you—you stole that magazine from me!"

"That first class." Ben nodded with a chagrined smile. "I was terrified you'd recognize me. I wasn't sure you'd seen me at Necessitas when you'd walked by—"

"So, are you telling me it was all a setup?" Hally's voice was tight.

"Lou Jay's gourmet class? No, that was a coincidence." His green eyes glinted. "Or fate. Take your pick."

"But the rest—you were toying with me, making me believe—" Hally regarded him, her cheeks flaming with indignation and anger. "If you think I'm going to be one of your—your trophies—well, you don't know me very well," she said haughtily.

Now, Ben looked thoroughly bewildered. "Trophies? Hally, I don't know what you're—"

"Maybe Veronica Wilmott's okay with that sort of thing, but I'm not," she blustered.

"What sort of thing? Do you think—oh, wow." Ben shook his head. "Veronica and I are not—"

"Monique's throwing the bouquet!" A young woman bulldozed between them.

"Well?" Ben cocked an eyebrow at her, stepping back. "You going to try your luck?"

Hally emptied her champagne glass and placed it on the table. She didn't believe in luck—or this silly ritual. Besides, marriage was a complication she didn't need right now. She was an advertising executive; her life had no room for romance and—

The bouquet arced above the scrabbling hands and hit Hally squarely on the chest. Her arms reflexively clamped around it. The woman standing next to her flashed her a sour look.

"It's fate," Ben whispered in her ear.

Hally stared at the bouquet in her hands, dazed.

"Who—? Hally! Hally you caught it!" Monique clapped her hands joyously.

Hally withered and blushed under the crowd's stare.

"Whoohoo, Ben! You better run, man!" shouted a male voice.

"I'm not running anywhere," stated Ben, wrapping a possessive arm around Hally.

Hally's eyes were poisonous. "Get away from me," she hissed through gritted teeth.

Ben dropped his arm, took her hand gruffly and led her away from the crowd.

"Where are you taking me? Let go—"

Ben pushed her into the kitchen. Lou Jay and two of his helpers looked up.

"Ah! Ben, Hally. My two Gourmet Hearts!" Lou Jay put his hands on his hips, a stern look spreading across his large, fleshy face. "But you both deceived me. Monique tells me, Ben, that you are not an Atkinson, after all. And you—" He pointed a sausagelike finger at Hally.

"Me? But I didn't deceive you," protested Hally.

"Certainly, you did. You told me you were not looking for romance." He broke out into a smile, threw back his head, and laughed. "But I know people, yes, I do."

"Lou Jay? Is there somewhere private where—?"

"Come with me." Lou Jay snatched up Hally's hand and led them to the freezing unit.

"I'm not staying in here," said Hally, turning around. But Lou Jay had already closed the door.

"Hally, we have to set a few things straight," began Ben.

Hally pulled down the handle. The door didn't budge. "Hey! We're locked in here!"

"Number one: I didn't tell you who I really was because I knew you were working on the Bel Abner campaign." Ben took a breath. "I didn't want to influence you—or be influenced *by* you."

"You're telling me I got this account on my own?" said Hally, looking dubious.

"Trust me. When it comes to the family business my opinion doesn't even come into play."

"Then why'd you come that night?"

Ben rolled his lips between his teeth. "The same reason I enrolled in that gourmet class. I've finally conceded to honor my father's wishes, and immerse myself in the family business. And now that I've seen what it's all about, well, you could say it's piqued my interest."

"I'm happy for you," she grumbled sarcastically, and

The Gourmet Cupid 181

pounded on the freezer door. "Lou Jay! Let us out!" She rubbed her arms. "It's freezing in here."

"Here." Ben draped his tuxedo jacket over her shoulders. She went to shrug it off, but Ben stopped her. "Wait a second, will ya? Give me a chance to finish."

"Okay, you've got two minutes before I start screaming."

Ben gave her an exasperated look. "Number Two: Veronica Wilmott is *not* one of my . . . 'trophies.' I have known her since I was six years old. Okay, at one time we were romantically involved—but that was over a long time ago."

"But you shared a room at the Kingsdale Hotel," said Hally, her heart thumping wildly in her chest.

"We had two separate rooms—not even on the same floor. And that night at the Arbre? Veronica just happened to show up just minutes before you did." Ben sighed. "Okay, I'm aware that Ronnie, well . . . still fancies me some. But the feeling is not, and will never be, mutual."

Hally regarded him, her doubt slowly waning. Was he telling the truth?

"Number Three:—"

"Okay, okay. I admit I made a few wrong assumptions—"

"Shut up, will you?" Ben's sudden impassioned look took Hally aback. She stood, rooted to her spot, her amber eyes locked onto his.

"Number Three: I am deeply, deeply, utterly, and insanely crazy about you."

Hally blinked.

"I can't stop thinking about you, Hally. When I was in L.A., all I could think about was you: what is Hally doing now? I wondered. Is she putting her hair up in that silly braid? Is she tugging on her earlobe, the way she does when she's thinking or when's she's nervous? Is she cooking herself a half-decent meal? Or is she defrosting one of those dinners in her little freezer?'' Ben raked his fingers through his hair. ''I called you every day, until one day you actually answered. But I was suddenly so tongue-tied I had to hang up.''

Hally couldn't imagine this man, this handsome, suave man, ever being too nervous to speak.

''I—I've been thinking about you, too. Or rather, trying not to,'' she admitted, glancing down at her dyed-green pumps.

Ben took a step toward her so that the tips of his shoes touched hers. He cupped her chin and lifted her face to his.

''Haven't you figured it out yet? I'm in love with you,'' he whispered gently. ''I love you, Hally Christina Chrisswell.''

Hally closed her eyes as his lips brushed the tip of her nose, then hungrily sought her mouth.

''I love you, too, Ben,'' she murmured throatily.

''Ah! I am sorry to interrupt my Gourmet Hearts, but I was afraid you might turn into icicles in here,'' said Lou Jay, poking his head around the door.

''Don't worry about us, Lou Jay.'' Ben drew Hally closer. ''We've got enough heat to keep this romance burning. Between us we've got 196 degrees.''

''And two Gourmet Hearts,'' added Hally with a laugh.